DOUBLE DANGER

'He knew who you were!' Belinda repeated. She scanned the length of the street, but Justin was gone. 'You realise what that means?'

Another clue. Another piece of solid evidence. The mystery was beginning to take shape.

'It means he's lying again,' Holly said. 'The doctor's wrong. The police are wrong. He's a fake!' she cried.

'Exactly!' Tracy's face nearly split into two with smiling so hard.

'But it's not quite that simple,' said Belinda. 'Now he knows Holly knows!' she explained. 'He just recognised her as the girl who was there when he was crashing his car. He knows she knows too much!'

Holly felt the words trickle like ice into her brain. She knew from the start Justin Mason spelled danger. Now he recognised her as the person who had seen his crime.

That felt like danger to Holly. That felt like double danger!

GW00726109

The Mystery Club series

Double Danger
The Mystery Club 2

Fiona Kelly

*Hodder
Children's
Books*

a division of Hodder Headline plc

Special thanks to Jenny Oldfield

Copyright © Ben M. Baglio 1993

Created by Ben M. Baglio
London W6 0HE

First published in Great Britain in 1993
by Knight Books

A Catalogue record for this book is available from the
British Library

ISBN 0 340 58868 3

Typeset by
Hewer Text Composition Services, Edinburgh

Printed and bound in Great Britain by
Cox & Wyman Ltd, Reading, Berkshire

Hodder Children's Books
A Division of Hodder Headline plc
338 Euston Road
London NW1 3BH

To Dan Weiss, a wonderful teacher

1 Eighty miles an hour

It was chaos at home as usual, so Holly Adams was out on her bike. Builders and electricians and joiners had taken over the house and some man with a beer belly and jeans halfway down his bum was scrambling under the sink to fix the plumbing. Then she had to answer phone calls from her mother at the office; had the builder rung the double-glazing man yet? Did the electrician remember to fix the dimmer switch in the lounge? Her sensible dad was away selling his hand-carved furniture. Only Jamie was at home, 'helping' the builders. Home sweet home.

So Holly took off on her bike. Happy holiday! No school, no hassle, not even any Mystery Club meetings. Just a bike ride over the moor on a peaceful sunny day. She let go of the brakes on a downhill stretch, hair flying free, feeling the warmth on her face.

Trouble was the last thing Holly Adams wanted today, but like iron filings to a magnet, it found her. Out here, riding free along the ridge of the moorside, with Willow Dale spread out like an *A to Z* below, a black bullet shape roared past her at eighty miles an hour. It came and was gone in a hot, mean rush.

'Idiot!' Holly wobbled and fell sideways into bilberry bushes. Sitting there, she swore loudly. The driver was a tanned man in dark glasses and a white open-necked shirt. She'd caught sight of him leering sideways at her as he forced her off the road.

Gingerly, Holly stood up. 'Oh, no!' she groaned. Blue juice from the berries had stained her T-shirt, and her front wheel had lost a couple of spokes. She got back on her bike, shaky and angry. As she wobbled along again, Holly planned an article for Steffie Smith, editor of *Winformation*, the school magazine: 'Cyclists Call for Safety. End of the Road for Lunatic Motorists!'

But her plan for revenge soon went smash. She rounded a bend, saw the black car swoop into the dip and take the next hill with a throaty roar. She heard the brakes, saw it leave the road, rear up over the banking and tear through a dry-stone wall.

With fear gripping her throat, Holly took the descent and pedalled like mad up the next hill, in time to see the car still lurching over rough purple heather. By now it was out of control. It hit a rock on the skyline with a sickening crunch and slewed sideways. Spinning like a toy, it disappeared over the edge.

Holly felt her heart flip. She dropped her bike and ran towards the outcrop of rocks. The heather pulled and tripped her, but she staggered on. A worker raced out of a nearby barn, running with Holly towards the noise. They reached the crag together. The man caught Holly's arm. 'Stop!' he yelled.

She looked down. There was a sheer edge. The rock fell into nothing. Steadying themselves, the man and Holly peered down at the car fifty feet below. It was turned on its back like a helpless beetle, wheels still spinning. The man breathed in sharply. Holly held on to him. What she noticed, after the screeching brakes, the scraping metal, the crunching, the sliding and the smashing, was the complete silence. A curlew rose from the heather and soared overhead.

'Stay here!' the man said to Holly. He started to scramble diagonally down the cliff, using a sheep track. He grabbed clumps of coarse grass and found footholds on the steep slope. Below, the wheels of the car still spun in the eerie silence.

No way am I stopping here! Holly thought. She

set off after him. Less strong, but more agile, she soon caught him up. They reached the bottom together.

'Steady on.' The farm worker gasped for breath. 'It's dangerous. We should go back . . . Get help.' They looked at the battered shell of the car, its windows blank and crazed, its tyres spinning gently.

'No!' Holly thought of the driver. 'He needs help now. Let's go.' She tugged at the man's sleeve, pulling him forward through the long grass.

'The whole thing could go up in flames,' the man warned.

Holly nodded, but she knew they'd have to take the risk.

The slow click-click-click of the turning wheels broke the silence. They were near enough to try the driver's door.

Jammed. The shell was so buckled out of shape that none of the doors would open. Frantically they pulled. The driver was in there injured; unconscious or worse.

The man pushed Holly back. They were sweating and scratched from the brambles. 'It's no use. We need help.'

Holly nodded this time and gasped out, 'Go and ring the police. I'll stay.' She squatted by the smashed car, her nerves steadying, determined to wait.

The man glanced once at her stubborn face, then nodded and ran off. He scrambled up the ledge, out of sight.

The sun beat down and the place smelt of petrol and smouldering tyres. It could all go up in flames, like the man said. The stupid wheels turned on. *I have to do something*, Holly thought.

She had to try to open the bashed metal cage. She just wanted to let the driver see someone was here to help. But trying to see through the crazy pattern of splintered safety glass was impossible.

Holly thought at the speed of light. True, she couldn't open a door, but she could push through a shattered window and gain access that way. There were stones, hand-sized stones, everywhere. Holly grasped one, chose the passenger side window, took a deep breath and hammered. The dull thud of disintegrating safety glass sounded sinister. Holly drew breath. She chipped away at the glass until she could peer inside.

It was dark. The petrol smell made her sick and faint. Or was it dread? She looked for a body, pale faced, twisted; maybe bloody, maybe dreadfully disfigured. But nothing moved. There was nothing in the driver's seat, nothing on the floor, or flung by the impact into the back seat. There was nothing at all in the car.

Holly pulled her face out of the darkness into sunlight. 'Nothing!' She gave a hollow laugh. It wasn't funny. *Make sure*, she told herself. It defied common sense.

She looked again, but there was still no one in the car. It didn't just crash itself. Locked in her memory was the man in dark glasses speeding down the road.

Horror crept back in.

Suppose he was thrown out. Suppose a door was flung open as the car hit the cliff edge. There would be a body somewhere on the cliff, or down here in what looked now like a disused quarry, with sheer sides all around, and boulders littering the bottom. *There'll be a body*, Holly told herself over and over. She squatted at a safe distance and began to shiver in the midday sun.

Suddenly the day was ripped apart by a boom of metal and a roar of flames. The car exploded. Holly flattened herself behind a boulder. Bits of glass and metal flew in all directions and black smoke billowed overhead in a mushroom cloud as flames enveloped the wreck.

The farm worker came running back with his father. 'Luke, you see if the girl's OK!' the older man yelled.

'You OK?' he asked Holly. She nodded.

The police cars and Land Rovers roared to the scene within minutes. The cliff top swarmed with uniforms. Firemen's hoses snaked down into the quarry, and men with radio phones and huge steel claws and winding gear to prise the car open.

Holly watched the men douse the flames. 'There's no one in there,' she told them. 'It's empty.'

A fireman gave her a stern look and went on with the job.

'I looked,' Holly told Luke. 'I broke a window. There's no one in there.'

Luke shook his head, watching intently.

'Get the girl out of here,' a man in uniform ordered. He clearly thought Holly couldn't take the strain.

'No, I'm OK,' Holly protested. She'd seen it through this far, hadn't she?

'He's right,' Luke said quietly. 'There's no need for us to stick around any longer.' He took Holly by the hand.

'Maybe the driver got thrown out. He's probably lying injured!' she protested again.

'That's their business, not ours,' he told her. 'We've done our bit.' He was gentle, but he led her firmly from the scene of the accident, back up the cliff to his house, where his mother gave Holly endless cups of tea, and they waited.

The police found nothing. They searched the burnt-out wreck, the quarry, the cliff and the scarred heather. They came to the farmhouse with the news; the driver was nowhere to be found.

Holly gave them a description of the man who had so mysteriously vanished. Age: around 30. Hair: dark and combed back. Clothes: white shirt, dark glasses. 'That fits,' the policewoman said. 'With the type of car he was driving, I mean. We're checking the computer for ownership now.' She wrote down everything Holly had described.

'He was speeding,' Holly told her finally.

The policewoman nodded again. 'Quite likely.'

'What do you think happened to him?'

The woman shrugged, then switched to a more formal style. 'We're continuing our investigations,' she said.

Back home at Holly's cottage, it all came on the evening news: 'Driver missing after moor top crash.' The police were appealing for further witnesses.

A reporter from the *Willow Dale Express* rang, wanting to interview Holly, but her mother refused. 'No, I'm sorry she's much too tired,' Mrs Adams said in her brisk, bank manager voice. She put the phone down firmly.

'Thanks, Mum!' Holly pulled a face. 'Are you a spoilsport, or what?' Holly loved everything about interviews and articles for newspapers, and wanted to be a journalist herself. Her mum had just put her out of a good piece of the action and the chance to meet a real live reporter.

'No. I'm a sensible mum who knows best!' Mrs Adams said. 'Newspapers always get hold of things and twist them about. Anyway, you are tired.'

'After my ordeal?' But Holly knew when to give in. She smiled, despite her disappointment. 'Can I just ring Tracy and Belinda?' she pleaded. The whole town had heard about the mysterious accident, but no one knew that she, Holly Adams, was the chief witness. Did she have a story to tell the Mystery Club!

'How many times have I heard those words!' her mother said with a laugh. She paused, then relented. 'I suppose . . .'

Holly gave her a grin and a hug, then made a grab for the phone.

'Wow! I'll be right there!' Tracy squealed, as soon as Holly told her the news. 'Wow!' She slammed down the receiver.

'I'll get my mum to drive me right down,' Belinda said. 'And don't you dare tell Tracy a single word until I get there!'

They arrived together, Tracy with her short blonde hair, grinning with excitement. Belinda, slower, heavier, but with her usual eye for mystery. Tracy was breathless and wanted to know everything all at once so she could figure it out first. Belinda took it in slowly, turned it over, and frowned through her wire-rimmed glasses. Together again, the Mystery Club. Holly, Tracy and Belinda, ace detectives of the Winifred Bowen-Davies School, always together, always sniffing out mysteries, never happy unless they had one to solve. Holly, the one who suspected murder around every corner. Tracy, who charged at problems like an Amazon, brave and determined. Belinda, who might look a lazy mess in her jeans and sweatshirt, but who had a razor-sharp brain. The Mystery Club.

And this was another real chance to prove themselves. They'd come a long way since Holly, new to Willow Dale, had advertised for fellow mystery enthusiasts in the school magazine. True, only Belinda and Tracy had turned up to the meeting, but they'd made the best crime solving team ever. To others they might look like three ordinary school-girls, and they had a long way to go to per-suade people like teachers, police and parents to take them seriously, but *they* knew how good they were when a mystery jumped up and grabbed them.

Mrs Adams brought three hot chocolates up to Holly's room. The three girls were sitting in a triangle on Holly's bed.

'Don't tire her out!' Mrs Adams warned as she shut the door on them.

'We won't!' they chorused, ignoring her of course.

'So?' Belinda demanded, leaning forward.

'So what?' Holly was enjoying their suspense.

'So a guy can't vanish into thin air!' cried Tracy.

'Well, I hate to say it, but I think we've got another mystery on our hands!' Holly said. She smiled.

'Let's go up there tomorrow and search for clues!' Tracy suggested, all action as usual.

They agreed; it should be their first move.

'The police and fire engine moved the car,'

Holly said. 'But there are skid marks, the broken wall, all of that for us to look at.'

Belinda sat quietly for a moment. 'Was the car a write-off?' she asked finally, fiddling with the frayed hem of her jeans. 'A total write-off?'

Holly nodded. 'I'll say. It blew up into a million pieces!'

'Do you have any idea of how much a car like that is worth?' said Belinda. She paused for effect. 'I asked my dad when it came up on the news.'

'How much?' Tracy and Holly asked together.

'Thirty-five grand!'

Silence showed their astonishment.

'That's an awful lot of car!' Tracy said at last, half whistling.

'So?' Holly said. 'Am I thinking what you're thinking?'

'What am I thinking?' Tracy asked.

'You're thinking what Belinda was thinking when she told us about the thirty-five grand, right?' Holly's voice was a whisper now.

Their three heads leaned together. 'A set-up!' they cried.

'That's right,' declared Holly. 'A staged accident for thirty-five thousand pounds' worth of insurance money!'

'Prove it!' Jamie, Holly's little brother and professional pest, burst open the door.

Holly chucked a pillow at him. 'Scram! You know you're not supposed to listen at keyholes!'

'Prove it! Prove it!' Jamie jeered, dodging the pillow.

'Go boil your head, Jamie!' Tracy scowled.

But Belinda only blinked at him over her glasses. 'Oh, we will,' she told him. 'We most certainly will!'

2   *Forget all about it*

'That accident was no accident! It was a fake!'
Tracy told her mother next morning. 'The guy
faked it for the insurance money!' She reached
for the cornflakes packet, hungry after her early
morning run.

Mrs Foster was collecting empty plastic bottles,
cardboard boxes, loo rolls and other rubbish into
a plastic sack. She had to get ready for work. 'It's
OK for some people round here,' she moaned.

'What is?' Tracy tied up the neck of the sack
with a wire fastener.

'Some of us need to work.'

'So?'

'Some of us don't have time to waste inventing
stories about a fake accident.' Tracy had caught
her at a bad time. In a few minutes twelve kids
under five would be arriving at the nursery
Mrs Foster ran, to paint, colour and construct
castles out of cardboard and sticky tape.

'Inventing!' For once Tracy was speechless.

'Yes, making it up. You know, letting your imaginations run away with you again!' Mrs Foster grabbed the bag of rubbish.

'Again!' Tracy's mouth fell open.

'Yes. You and Belinda and Holly. Well, you can forget it. I heard all about it on the news while you were out. The driver turned up late last night, wandering through town, lost. The police picked him up.'

'So?' Tracy didn't like to fall behind with the news. She should have been more on the ball. 'What did the police decide?'

'They say he lost his memory. He got thrown out of the car and knocked on the head. He can't remember a thing about it. But he's safe. They took him home. Mystery over, OK?' Mrs Foster swung the door closed behind her.

'Who is he? What did he say?' Tracy stammered out to a swinging door. Too late. She stood there in the empty kitchen.

'Dad, will the insurance company still have to pay up on this Mason case?' Belinda had actually beaten Tracy to it and listened to the morning news. She chewed a piece of toast thoughtfully.

'What Mason case?' Mr Hayes, a high-powered international businessman, was in his office, faxing things to New York and Tokyo. 'Don't drop those crumbs on the fax machine!' he warned his daughter.

'You know, the car crash Holly saw yesterday. The driver turned up late last night. He lost his memory, otherwise he's OK. What about the insurance?'

Her dad wasn't paying much attention. He stood there in his suit, feeding another sheet of paper into the fax.

'Mason? Mason who?' He picked up the phone.

'Justin Mason, the car driver.'

'Oh, amnesia, is it? Hmm . . .' He tapped his fingers as he waited impatiently for the phone to connect.

'Will he still get the insurance money?'

'Yes,' Mr Hayes said simply.

'But anyone could do that! Crash a really expensive car on purpose and get the insurance company to pay up. Anyone could fake it!' Belinda couldn't believe that any sane company would part with thirty-five thousand pounds without arguing.

Mr Hayes nodded. 'Probably.' His call was connected. He put one hand over the receiver. 'But why?' He smiled kindly, shrugged, then turned his back on Belinda. It was clearly the end of the conversation. She trailed off back to the kitchen for more toast.

'Don't be silly, Holly!' Mrs Adams sighed. 'Why should anyone deliberately crash a beautiful car like that!'

'For the money, of course!' It was all there in the morning newspaper, together with a photo of the driver, but the fact of Justin Mason's amnesia was just beginning to sink in.

'Hmm . . .' Mrs Adams put on her lipstick, then combed her hair. 'Don't forget to ask the builder to order the extra stone for the extension,' she reminded Holly.

'Listen, Mum!' Holly went on. 'He crashes this car on a deserted country road. How? Why? Nobody knows. He disappears. Where? He turns up and says he's lost his memory. How convenient. And he can still claim the insurance money. Thirty-five thousand pounds!'

Mrs Adams put on her jacket and smoothed down her skirt. 'If your father rings, tell him I've booked a table at the Koh-i-noor for Saturday, will you?' She smiled and kissed Holly's cheek. 'OK?'

'Mum!'

'No time now, Holly. See you later.' And Mrs Adams sailed out of the house, leaving

Holly sitting there amongst the brick dust and the coils of electricity cables.

Jamie smiled in his told-you-so way. 'And it's your turn to wash the breakfast things, Miss Clever Clogs!' he declared, smirking.

Holly went on staring at the front page report. The place, the time, the name of the man in dark glasses. It was true, someone could lose his memory from a blow to the head; it happened all the time in the mystery books she read. Or the mind could just block things out after a very great shock. That was common, too. But still there was something here that just didn't add up. Something very wrong. Slowly she went upstairs to get dressed.

The Mystery Club met up at eleven outside the main entrance to the Willow Dale shopping mall.

'That's it then,' Holly said with a shrug of her shoulders. 'The driver turns up. No mystery.'

'What!' Tracy and Belinda cried in astonishment.

'What do you mean, that's it!' Tracy exclaimed.

Holly's face lit up. 'Ha, fooled you!'

'Gee!' Tracy sounded relieved.

'Wow!' Belinda mocked Tracy's American

accent. They jostled each other towards the nearest bench.

'Just for a moment there you had us worried. We thought you'd lost your nerve!' Tracy said. 'Just when we'd planned to revisit the scene of the crime, remember?'

'Me!' The news of Justin Mason's magical reappearance, unscathed except for his loss of memory, had only served to deepen the mystery as far as Holly was concerned. The problem was the usual one; what to do about it when you couldn't get adults to believe you.

'Ice cream?' Belinda suggested.

'You bet!' cried Holly and Tracy. Ice cream was the Mystery Club's favourite food, and they never missed an opportunity to indulge their passion.

Belinda went over to the ice cream van in the car park and brought back three chocolate-nut sundaes. They always thought better with an ice cream apiece.

'You're sure it's the right guy?' Tracy said, taking a spoonful of whipped cream. 'The one in the newspaper is the one you saw driving?'

'Looks like it,' Holly nodded. 'No switch of identity, no hidden corpse. Pity.' They wandered along by Annie's Tearoom and the other shops in Willow Dale's picturesque town centre.

'What about the stretch of road where he crashed?' Belinda asked. 'Is it a bad bend, or what?'

Holly licked. 'Not especially. It's up the hill by Farfield Farm, you know? Before you turn off to the right for the reservoirs. It bends, then it straightens out. He went off the road just after the bend, near a very convenient quarry!'

'Maybe the sun was in his eyes?' Belinda asked tentatively. To Holly's astonishment she was already finishing her sundae. Belinda's appetite was legendary.

Holly shook her head. 'Wrong direction. The sun was behind him.'

'Hmm . . .' They came to a halt together. 'Hey, look!' Tracy pretended to sound surprised and gestured dramatically at a nearby hill.

They'd arrived on the corner leading up to the local police station. Holly and Belinda nodded. Holly wolfed down the remains of her sundae and led the march up the hill. After all, she was the eye-witness, and she'd been the first to think up the fake crash theory. Now she would be the first to tell the police about the insurance fraud line of investigation.

Confidently they strode into the police station, up to the desk marked 'Inquiries'.

The policeman at the desk looked bored. 'Yes?'

he said, hardly looking up from the report he was typing at a computer terminal.

'Hello, I'm Holly Adams.' She flashed him a brilliant smile.

He nodded, immune to the smile, and went on typing.

'I'm the witness to the Justin Mason crash!' A long pause was filled by the regular click-click-click of the keyboard. 'You know, the case currently under investigation?' Her smile was beginning to waver. Belinda and Tracy gave her nods of encouragement.

He nodded again. 'The case is closed.' He flicked his left ear, as if swatting an invisible fly.

'Closed!' the three girls said all at once. 'It can't be!'

'It is.'

'Why?' Holly demanded.

The policeman sighed. 'Didn't you hear? The driver turned up last night. No passengers involved, no other vehicle, no suspicious circumstances. Case closed.'

'What about dangerous driving?' Holly declared. 'Or speeding, driving without due care and attention? Something!'

'No witnesses.' Still he went on typing.

'But *I* saw him. I'm a witness!' Holly was

incensed. Her voice had risen. Behind her, Tracy was tugging at her T-shirt.

'No corroboration from other witnesses, so there's no case to answer.' The policeman switched off the computer and wandered through a glass doorway. He started tidying his desk, looked up briefly at their amazed faces, then came back in and faced Holly across the desk.

'Listen, love, the doc's had a look at this Justin Mason character and confirmed the loss of memory. Trauma due to the crash, shock, that sort of thing. No one's hurt. No damage done, except to a bit of old stone wall.' He gave Holly an understanding wink. 'Best forget all about it, eh?'

Forget all about it! He obviously didn't know Holly Adams. 'No, listen, there's more to it than you think!' she insisted.

The policeman gave her a look. Tracy was tugging at her T-shirt even harder.

Holly surged on. 'He crashed the car on purpose to claim the insurance money. That car's worth thirty-five thousand pounds! He set it all up: the crash, the loss of memory, everything! It's a fraud!'

But by now the policeman's patience had snapped. He crossed his stocky arms, leaned back and stared steadily at Holly. 'A right little Agatha Christie, aren't we?'

'It's true; the whole thing's a fake!'

By now there was a queue behind the girls in the tiny reception room. The policeman warned Holly to keep her voice down.

A policewoman came out from the inner office. 'Hello,' she said with a smile. It was the same officer who'd taken Holly's statement at Farfield Farm. 'Would you like to come through?'

Holly gave Tracy and Belinda a significant look and led them into the office. *Now we're getting somewhere*, she told herself. The policewoman noted down everything Holly said. She smiled all the time she was writing. She looked up, still smiling. 'You know who the driver is?' she asked. The question was obviously loaded.

'Justin Mason,' Holly stammered. 'Of course.' For some reason she bluffed her way through the answer.

'Of the Mason family,' the woman said very distinctly, stressing the word 'the'.

Holly nodded, while Tracy fiddled with her hair and Belinda went red. 'The Mason family; oh, yes, of course,' Holly said slowly, all the while wondering just who the Masons were.

The woman's smile stretched further. She shrugged slightly. 'So it goes without saying, doesn't it, that Justin Mason is the last person in this town who would need to crash his car just so he could claim the insurance money?' She waited briefly for them to nod and agree. 'Why would someone with his background take such a risk? Why would he need to?'

It was terrible, Holly thought. The policewoman was being so nice, like a teacher giving them a second chance to hand in their homework. She was young and sympathetic, but she was definitely telling them to get lost. The three girls wished the ground would swallow them.

The policewoman kindly asked Holly if she'd recovered from yesterday's ordeal. 'I know it's a terrible shock to witness a crash like that.'

'No, I'm fine, thanks,' Holly insisted.

'You might think so, but people sometimes get delayed shock.' She smiled at Holly. 'Be sure and get plenty of rest,' she said.

They nodded and let themselves be led out, looking sheepish, past the policeman and the people in the queue. 'Goodbye,' they said to the smiling policewoman, 'and thank you very much!'

They stood outside the station, blinking in the sunlight.

'*Thank* you!' Tracy exploded. 'For what?' English

politeness still drove her crazy, even after all these years.

'The Mason family?' Belinda repeated, shaking her head.

'Who on earth are the Mason family?' Tracy yelled.

Holly took a deep breath and confessed. 'I don't know.'

'You don't know!' Tracy was speechless.

'Sorry.' Holly knew she had let them down. Her nerve had weakened under the force of the policewoman's politeness.

'Never mind,' Belinda said. 'These Masons are obviously well known around here. And they're rich.'

'So they're powerful too,' Tracy figured.

'So no one will believe us,' Holly said. For a second she felt weak and helpless. Then she pulled herself together. One mistake wasn't the end of the world. 'Unless we prove it all ourselves!' she told them.

'Just what we need to liven up our holiday,' Tracy said. 'A good mystery!'

They took a deep breath and went back to square one. 'So, who is this Justin Mason?' asked Holly. 'That's the first thing.' She began listing things on her fingers. 'And why wasn't it included in the newspaper report, eh?'

Belinda cut right in with, 'If he's rich and powerful, my dad will know him!'

And they rushed straight up to her house, to catch Mr Hayes before he jetted off on his next business trip.

3 The Manor House

Mr Hayes sighed at his daughter's appearance on their front lawn. Holly saw him sigh, and she had to agree that the lawn was better groomed; the horse, the house, the cleaning lady were all better groomed than Belinda. She went careering across the neatly mown area, dressed in that same old green sweatshirt. No wonder he'd sighed.

'Dad!' Belinda cried. 'Wait!' He was climbing into his champagne-coloured executive saloon.

The girls arrived breathless and geared up for something important. 'Two minutes,' he said, tapping his watch. 'That's all I can spare.'

'Right.' Belinda drew breath. She was used to having a successful international businessman for a father. She knew she had to slot into his busy schedule.

'Really, you're so out of condition,' Tracy said, pushing her way in. 'Mr Hayes, we need some vital information from you!'

'About Justin Mason,' Holly cut in.

'Don't all talk at once.' They all crowded round the open car door and he retreated further into its cream leather interior. 'Now what do you want to know?'

'Who's Justin Mason?' they all said at once.

'Easy,' he said. 'He's the son of Eddie Mason, the man who owns most of Yorkshire's daily and weekly newspapers. Justin is the only son. The wife's dead, a long time since. Eddie Mason's one of the most important men in Yorkshire.'

'Rich?' Tracy asked.

'Very.' Mr Hayes was smiling, but discreet. He didn't like talking about money. He had too much of it himself.

'How rich?' Tracy wanted to know.

'He owns six or seven newspapers, a yacht in Monaco, a villa in Tuscany, and the big house up the hill.'

The girls gasped.

'*That* rich!' Tracy whistled.

'Which house?' Holly asked.

'The Manor House.' With that, Mr Hayes shut the car door, relaxed into the upholstery and purred off down the drive.

'And don't forget to exercise that horse!' he yelled at Belinda through the electronically controlled window.

'OK, OK,' she yelled back. He didn't need to nag her about her horse. She never forgot Meltdown; he should know that.

'What's the Manor House?' Tracy asked. 'Does it mean lord of the manor, medieval-type stuff?'

'Yes.' Belinda slowly put two and two together. 'It's one of the oldest houses in Willow Dale. Mason? Of course, Masons of the Manor House!' It was a common name and she only just made the connection. She could kick herself. 'Built in the seventeenth century, a massive place. Mullioned windows, huge garden.'

'Wow!' Tracy was impressed.

'But not so huge as it used to be,' Belinda went on. 'The present owner, Edward Mason, the newspaper tycoon, sold off some of the land to builders about twenty years ago. Actually, we're standing on a bit of it now!'

'You mean your house is built on Manor House land?' Holly looked up at Belinda's enormous chalet-style home. 'You mean you're Justin Mason's actual neighbour!' Why on earth hadn't she said so before?

Belinda coughed with embarrassment. 'Looks like it.' They glared at her. 'How should I know? I suppose both of you know all your neighbours, then?'

'You're unbelievable!' Tracy moaned.

'Mason's a common name,' Belinda protested.

It was pointless to argue. 'At least you can show us where it is,' Tracy finished off.

They trooped up the lane after Belinda. The higher up the hill they went, the more expensive the houses became, with bigger cars in the drive. Finally they came to an ancient stone gatepost crowned with lions. Beyond that was a driveway lined with lavender bushes, leading up to a paved courtyard and a house covered with ivy, stone carvings and dovecotes.

The Manor House. What was left of the gardens was still enough to fit in roughly six of Holly's cottages.

'Seriously rich,' Holly noted.

'Hey, over here!' Tracy waved them across to the ancient stone boundary wall. They followed it round until it brought them close enough to the house to see two huge Great Danes lying asleep in the stone doorway, and the flower-beds full of white and red roses.

'Peaceful,' Holly whispered.

'Quaint,' Tracy agreed.

'It just shows why the police believed this Justin Mason,' Belinda put in.

'Who'd suspect anyone living here of deliberately smashing even a china teacup?' Holly said. 'Let alone thirty-five grand's worth of car!'

Snip-snip went a pair of secateurs right under their noses. The girls bobbed down out of sight. *Snip-snip.* A gardener's wrinkled face appeared over the wall, dead heading roses. 'Hey!' he said when he spotted them crouching by the wall. 'Hey, you lot!'

They shot off down the lane, to the half-hearted barking of two sun-dazed Great Danes.

Less than an hour later the girls had reverted to their original plan. They were out on their bikes, revisiting the scene of the crime.

'Say, this is really something!' Tracy shook her head as they pedalled three abreast. The view of Willow Dale spread out below was spectacular.

'Whose idea was this anyway?' Belinda fell behind as they reached the steepest part of the hill up on to the moor side.

'God, you're so unfit!' Tracy jeered. 'Serves you right for letting that horse of yours carry you everywhere.'

'I'll have you know that horse riding is a very energetic sport!' Belinda's glasses were steaming up. 'Everyone admits that. Horsewomen have to be superbly fit. Every muscle toned to perfection!' Her lungs had begun to ache. The hill stretched on forever.

'Says you!' Tracy laughed, sailing ahead.

'Shh, I'm trying to think,' said Holly.

'I'm glad someone is,' Belinda moaned. 'Anyway, this had better be worth it.' They reached the top at last. 'Go on, Holly, explain exactly what we're doing here!'

They got off their bikes and looked along the road that snaked its way through the heather along the ridge of the moor.

'One, we're revisiting the scene of the crime, like we agreed,' Holly said.

'Alleged crime,' Belinda muttered.

Holly ignored her and pulled out the red Mystery Club notebook. 'Which at a rough guess is a good half-mile from here, over past the farm, just round the first bend, OK?'

They set off again, pedalling more easily along the ridge. 'Here is where the car forced me off the road, right?' Holly recognised the very bushes.

'Stop!' The others obeyed. 'Now, we're going to measure some speeds and distances.'

Tracy's eyebrows shot up. 'My brain is already beginning to hurt!'

'That's why we use a calculator!' Belinda said, pulling a small calculator out of her pocket. Holly had asked her to bring it along. Belinda waved it at Tracy. 'This is called the on/off button, see?'

'Shh, I'm thinking!' Holly asked Belinda to time her. 'I'll pedal from here to the hole in the wall where Justin Mason's car went through. You time how long it takes me, OK?'

Belinda nodded. 'Fair enough. Then what?'

'Then Tracy has to use her pedometer to cover the same distance on foot.'

'Her *what*?' Belinda blinked.

'Pedometer. You strap it to your leg to measure the exact distance you run. For jogging or whatever.'

'Trust you to have one of those!' Belinda said, shaking her head at Tracy.

'She likes me really,' Tracy teased. 'But to be honest, I don't see why you asked me to bring it along, Holly.'

'Shh!' Holly said.

'We know – you're thinking!' Tracy and Belinda laughed.

'So then we'll have the time and the distance.' Holly was trying to be clear. She jotted down some notes in the Mystery Club book, then stuffed it back into her jeans pocket.

'Let's do it!' Tracy was off, pedometer strapped to her leg. As usual, she was all for getting down to action. Besides, she'd arranged to meet her boyfriend, Kurt Welford, at seven.

'OK?' Holly set off pedalling while Belinda timed her.

At the end, they sat on the heap of broken

stones, next to the gash in the wall made by Justin Mason's car. Belinda entered some figures on her calculator. 'Twelve miles per hour,' she said. 'That's your speed on the bike.'

'Now,' Holly said. 'I reckon Justin Mason was doing eighty.'

'Make that sixty,' Tracy corrected. Holly had a tendency to exaggerate.

'OK, sixty.' She glanced at Belinda. 'So, how long should it have taken him to drive this stretch of road?'

'Thirty seconds,' Belinda said, looking at her calculator.

'And how long did it take me on my bike?'

'Two and a half minutes.'

The girls sat and looked at one another, eyes glinting. 'Yet I got here in time to see the car vanish over the edge of the quarry!' Holly said. 'How long for a car to cover the last couple of hundred yards over rough heather?'

'Fifteen seconds at most,' Belinda guessed.

'See!' Holly grabbed their arms. 'It doesn't add up! I knew it wouldn't! Forty-five seconds after throwing me off the bike, he should already have been down there at the bottom of that quarry! Not two and a half minutes, nothing like!'

'He must have stopped,' Tracy said.

'Yeah, stopped to set the car at the right angle

down this last bit of road. Then he'd still have time to hop out, release the handbrake, watch the empty car gather speed and crash through the wall. Time to watch it go over the edge!' Belinda painted the full picture.

'And time to hide over the other side of the wall when he saw me pedalling like mad to reach the scene. Then he headed off to town to fake his amnesia!' Holly could hardly speak for excitement.

'Holly, you're a genius!' Tracy jumped up and hugged her. 'You're a complete genius!'

'You should tell that to my maths teacher,' Holly said, grinning.

'Great,' Belinda agreed. 'This is solid evidence that the car didn't just skid on the gravel and crash. Great!'

'It's a start,' Holly admitted. But false modesty wasn't really her style. She leapt on top of the heap of stones and held up her arms like a footballer who'd just scored a goal. 'In fact it's totally terrific!' she shouted, punching the sky.

4 Double danger

Tracy saw Kurt waiting outside Annie's Tearoom at seven on the dot. She smiled and waved. Kurt was tall, good looking and a year older. She ran to meet him. They had half an hour before his cricket practice, and she knew all he'd want to talk about was bowling tactics and batting techniques. She didn't mind. She could switch off her brain and dream about the new mystery.

'Hi!' Kurt kissed Tracy on the cheek.

They followed the waitress to a table by the window, and ordered a Coke and a milkshake. The room was decorated in an old-fashioned style: stained glass windows, marquetry hunting scenes in huge frames on the wall, rows of curious antique teapots on heavy wooden shelves. Tracy liked it. 'Olde Englishe', she called it in her letters to her friends back home in the States.

'What's new?' Kurt asked.

'Nothing much.' The Mystery Club had made it a rule never to discuss details of current cases. 'Holly saw a car crash up on the moor yesterday, that's all.' She tried to sound off-hand.

'Yeah? That's right, I read about it.'

'You feel sorry for the car, I bet!' Tracy teased. 'All that lovely metal gone up in flames! What about poor Holly?'

'She OK?' Kurt asked.

'Of course.' Tracy finished joking and smiled brilliantly. 'So tell me about your last cricket match.' She knew that would be good for a full five minutes of off-spinners and googlies, and give her a chance to gaze around the tearoom.

She nearly choked on her milkshake. She looked, and she looked again. First she was sure, then she wasn't sure, then there was no doubt in her mind. Sitting across the room in a quiet corner reserved for smokers was Justin Mason!

'Kurt!' Tracy grabbed his arm. 'Shh! Look over there. Who do you think that is?'

'Who? A film star or what?' he said. There was only a smooth-looking man sitting chatting cosily to a woman with long legs and flame-coloured hair.

'It's Justin Mason!' Tracy said, nearly bouncing off her chair. 'Don't you recognise him?'

'*Who*?'

'Justin Mason! The guy who smashed up his car.' Tracy took another look. Justin and his companion were caught up in conversation, her head leaning close up to his dark grey jacket.

'Steady on.' Kurt raked through his memory. 'Yeah, it does look like him,' he confirmed. 'Who's she, then?'

'Trust you,' Tracy said. The woman was dressed in a bright yellow top, white jeans and little gold shoes. She wore lots of gold jewellery and seemed incredibly vain. 'I've never seen her before,' Tracy said.

'He's none the worse for wear, anyway.' Kurt watched Justin Mason lean over and kiss his girlfriend.

'Amnesia,' Tracy told him. 'A complete blackout. Can you believe it?'

Kurt shook his head. 'He seems fine to me.' Now Justin Mason was stroking the woman's cheek, smiling and saying soft words. They seemed oblivious of everyone else in the cafe.

'Got it!' Tracy said with a gasp.

'What? Got what?' Kurt looked at his watch. 'Hey listen, I've got to go. I'm going to be late.' He stood up.

'No!' Tracy knew she had to seize this opportunity. The Mystery Club suspect was actually sitting across the room, and she had something very important to test out.

'Listen Kurt, just stay here and keep an eye on those two, would you? I've got to make a phone call.'

Kurt sat down. 'OK, but be quick.' He looked awkwardly at Tracy. 'It's just that I need to get to this practice, see. I don't want to lose my place in the first team.'

'Two minutes!' she promised, and headed for the phone booth. She quickly punched in Holly's number. Jamie answered and said Holly was at Belinda's. She rang Belinda's. Her mother said they were both out in the stable.

Tracy looked back into the tearoom to see if Justin Mason was still there, but he was out of sight. All she could see was Kurt looking impatient. 'Could you go fetch her, Mrs Hayes? It's urgent.'

'Hang on, I'll put you through,' Mrs Hayes said. They had an extension out into the stable.

As soon as Belinda picked up, Tracy sprang her message on them: 'Drop everything! Get yourselves down here fast. I'm in Annie's. I'll explain later!' Then she walked nonchalantly back to the table.

45

'OK?' Kurt said.

She darted a look at Justin Mason's corner; they were still there.

'Two more kisses and a fondle,' Kurt reported. He grinned and blushed as he said it.

Tracy laughed.

'Listen, I've got to go. Queen and country, you know!' Kurt stood to attention.

'Cricket!' Tracy groaned.

He backed away under the row of teapots, still grinning. He gave a little wave. 'See you.'

Tracy nodded and sat there alone sipping her milkshake and glancing at her watch. One minute, two minutes, three. Justin Mason asked for the bill. His girlfriend trotted off to the Ladies. Five whole minutes. Tracy groaned. Where were Holly and Belinda?

Justin stood up as his girlfriend came back. He helped her on with her shiny green jacket, picked up the bill and headed for the cash desk. Too late. The Mystery Club had missed their golden opportunity!

Justin paid the bill, put his arm round his girlfriend and led her to the door between the walnut cakes and the ginger parkin.

Just then Holly swung open the door and dashed in from the street, Belinda close behind.

Justin stepped back out of the way. Holly muttered her thanks, then stopped dead in her tracks. She stood in the doorway, face to face with Justin Mason.

It was a moment suspended in time. The surprise registered on Holly's face. Here he was, Justin Mason, in the flesh. He was standing just two feet away from her, his hair carefully styled back, his features small and even. His eyes were cold and calculating. It was the first time she'd seen his eyes.

The girlfriend stepped in between them and went out through the door in a blur of auburn and gold. Justin Mason hesitated, looking Holly straight in the face. His eyes narrowed and he pulled his mouth sideways. Holly was sure he was trying to place her. She tried to avoid his gaze, lowering her pale grey eyes. But he'd recognised her! He shot her a glance which said, *I know who you are. I know when I first saw you!*

The girlfriend waited impatiently out on the street. Justin pulled himself together, nodded at the cashier, and left.

Tracy raced across the thick green carpet to greet her friends. For a moment they were too excited to speak. Holly felt the full force of it, the face to face encounter with Justin Mason.

Until this moment, she'd only seen that face

behind a windscreen, or staring from a newspaper. Now in reality, she realised it was colder, harder, crueller than she'd ever imagined.

'He recognised you!' Tracy whispered. 'Absolutely no doubt about it!'

Holly nodded silently, still lost in thought.

'Can I help you?' the cashier asked. 'A table for three?'

Tracy shook her head and led the others out of the tearoom.

'He did know who you were!' Belinda repeated. She scanned the length of the street, but Justin and his girlfriend had gone. 'You realise what that means?'

Another clue. Another piece of solid evidence. Holly felt like a child joining up the numbered dots to make a picture to colour. The thing was beginning to take shape.

'It means he's lying again,' Holly said. 'If he knows who I am, it means he can't have lost his memory in the first place. The doctor's wrong. The police are wrong. He's a fake!' she cried.

'Exactly!' Tracy's spur of the moment plan had worked out well. Her face nearly split into two with smiling so hard.

'But it's still not quite that simple,' said Belinda.

'Why not?' Tracy asked, confused. It was time for congratulations, wasn't it?

'Because now he knows Holly knows!' Belinda explained. 'He just recognised her as the girl who was there when he was crashing his car. He knows she knows too much!'

Holly felt the words trickle like ice into her brain. She knew from the start Justin Mason spelled danger. First, he drove like a maniac, forcing her into a ditch. Now, he recognised her as the one person who had seen his crime.

That felt like danger to Holly. That felt like double danger!

5 Willow Dale 703611

'Yes, but he doesn't know who I am!' Holly repeated to herself in the bedroom mirror. Only when she was back in her room, surrounded by her familiar posters and photographs did the threat of Justin Mason begin to fade. She settled against her peach-coloured pillows, glad that her room at least was warm and cosy.

Belinda had been sweet. 'I understand if you don't want to get involved,' she'd said. 'You're the one who could be in danger here.'

Tracy had said, 'Anyhow, we're all in this together. You can count on us!'

They'd all put on brave faces and made their way home.

'So?' Holly asked her reflection now. 'He knows I know. But what can he do about it?' She squared her shoulders. The person who should really be rattled was Justin Mason. He was the one with something to hide.

She began her slow, careful finger count. One,

they knew he'd staged the crash and the loss of memory. Two, they knew that he was desperate for money. But why?

She attempted the question from all angles. Because his girlfriend likes expensive presents? Because a big business deal had fallen through? Because he's in debt and the bank won't lend him the money? Each answer fell flat. Why would someone from such a wealthy family need the money? What was thirty-five thousand pounds to a family with millions? Holly sat on her bed deep in thought.

Until Jamie burst in with a round of false machine-gun fire. Her carefully collected nerves shattered again.

'You're dead!' he crowed, flinging himself flat on his stomach, commando-style.

'And you will be – seriously – if you don't get out of here!' She threw a pen at him, but missed.

'Proved your case yet?' he taunted. 'Are you going to write it up for the school magazine?'

'Jamie, go away!' She scored a direct hit with her hairbrush, spiky side up.

'Ouch!'

'Jamie!' Mrs Adams yelled up a warning. 'Stop being a pest!'

Jamie skulked off.

'He's right, though!' Holly unexpectedly saw a chink of light. 'I never thought I'd say it, but he's right! I could report it – or pretend to!' She hauled herself up full height in front of the mirror; a tall, slender girl with a very determined look.

She went downstairs for the phone book, and soon found the number she wanted: Mason Newspaper Group, Head Office; Willow Dale 703611. She took the phone back to her room and dialled. She waited with held breath.

'Mason Newspapers,' a woman's voice said on the other end of the line.

Holly hesitated, summoning her courage.

'Can I help you?' the woman asked politely.

'I'm Holly Adams, from Winifred Bowen-Davies School. I'm working on an assignment for my English course.'

'Yes?' The voice sounded professional and patient.

'I wonder if it would be possible to meet Mr Mason for an interview?' Holly made her voice sound breathless and naive and as young as possible. She wanted to catch the woman's sympathy.

She rushed on. 'My teacher has asked us to do a newspaper interview with a local businessman or woman, and since Mr Mason is the most famous businessman in Willow Dale, and since he's involved in the newspaper business himself, I thought he would be the perfect person to ask. Do you think he would mind?'

There was a pause. The woman on the end of the phone sounded suitably amused, but impressed. 'Mr Mason is at home right now. Let me give him a ring for you. Can I have your name again?'

'Holly Adams.'

'Hold on please.'

Yes! Please say yes! Holly kept her fingers crossed. This was the plan that Jamie had put into her mind; a way of getting past those old stone walls of the Manor House, to see what she could find. She heard the receiver being picked up again.

'Hello, Miss Adams? I've spoken to Mr Mason, and he says that he could possibly spare half an hour tomorrow morning, before he goes off to London for several days. How would that be?'

'Terrific! I mean perfect. Thanks.' Holly uncrossed her fingers.

'Go to his house tomorrow morning then, at nine thirty. Ask for me. I'll be there.'

'Who are you, please?'

'I'm Rachel Stone. You know how to find us, don't you? We're at the Manor House on Moor Lane.'

'Yes, thank you. Oh, and Miss Stone . . .'

'Rachel.'

'Oh, Rachel, can I bring two friends along? We're all working on the assignment together. Do you think Mr Mason would mind?'

Rachel considered this latest request. 'No, I think that should be perfectly all right. Just remember though, Mr Mason is a busy man. He likes to help, especially young people interested in journalism; that's why I thought he would agree to meet you. However, you'll have just thirty minutes to ask your questions, so I'd write them down if I were you.'

'Yes, thank you, Miss . . . Rachel. Thank you!' Holly put down the phone. At that moment she could have hugged Jamie. The plan had worked perfectly!

Even Belinda made it for nine fifteen. Tracy and Holly called at her house on the way up, as arranged. 'Wear something smart,' Holly had warned her, so she turned up at the door with her hair scraped back in a ponytail; otherwise she'd made no concession to the importance of the occasion. Her jeans and sweatshirt would do.

'They'll throw you out!' Tracy said. 'They'll think you're the garbage man!'

'Not with my accent, they won't!' Belinda glared.

Tracy gave up. She'd never understand the English class system. Where she came from you always tried to look your best, so she was wearing the short plaid skirt and dark top she wore for orchestra concerts. Holly was looking smart and studious in her white embroidered blouse.

Bickering, they reached the stone entrance to the Manor House. How had three such different people come together as the Mystery Club, Holly wondered.

'What now?' Tracy asked.

As they hesitated at the gate, a woman came down the drive to meet them, the two Great Danes at her heels. She was English-rose pretty; slender, with light brown hair bobbed to chin length and pale skin. She shielded her face from the early sun, and as she came near, Holly saw she had small features and large hazel eyes.

'Which of you is Holly?' the woman said, smiling.

'I am.' Holly stepped forward, determined to deal coolly with the splendour and graciousness of all this.

'I'm Rachel Stone.' They shook hands. 'Mr

Mason's secretary. Which means general dogs-body!' Her laugh was light and pretty too.

She showed them into the house through a square hallway with dark ceiling beams. Oak doors led off in every direction, and a carved oak banister led upstairs to a landing decorated with wood panelling and rich red stained glass windows. Niches in the stone walls hoarded pieces of pewter and expensive blue and white china.

They went through into an office at the rear of the house. The room, which overlooked a patio and a lawn, was lined with old books, but it had a more modern feel. There was a computer terminal on a huge wooden desk, and there were at least three phones in the room. But the windows were leaded glass, and all the carved oak desks and tables smelt of lavender polish.

In awe of the grandeur, the girls stuck together in a little cluster on the central red patterned carpet while Rachel went off to fetch her boss.

'Gee!' Tracy said, sounding naive and easily impressed. 'Sorry.' She pulled herself together. 'It's just that I've never been inside a house like this before, except in the movies!'

Belinda, less overcome, felt her palms go sticky at the idea that somewhere under this roof Justin Mason himself lived. She shook her head. 'Don't you think this is just a tiny bit risky?' she said.

'Shh!' Holly turned to face the door as the handle clicked. 'Mr Mason?'

An elderly man in a dark suit stood there. He was tall and grey haired. He came towards them with a smile, but he could have been smiling at empty space. He shook hands like a politician.

'Enterprise, that's what I like!' he congratulated them. 'Young people with initiative!' He made himself comfortable behind the wide desk. The lamplight showed up the wrinkles; deep lines between his brows. But his voice sounded pleasant. 'And links between school and the community, I like that too.' He invited them to sit down.

Holly swallowed the lump in her throat and plunged in. 'Perhaps we could start with your own school, then? If we could just fill in a few biographical details first?' She got out her pen and the Mystery Club's red notebook.

'Quite.' He kept on smiling. 'It's the poor boy made good angle you're after, I expect. It makes a good story; rags to riches.' He glanced round the room at his possessions. 'Go on then, fire away!'

Holly asked the questions and Mr Mason answered them. Nothing it seemed would crack the veneer of the steady, respectable traditionalist who believed in hard work and determination. 'If you try hard enough, you can be anything you want to be,' he confided. 'I started doing obituaries and classified ads on the *Sheffield Star* over forty years ago, and look at me now. The old story. Hard work,' he said, drumming the desk with his fingers. 'Hard work and self-discipline. Would you believe I was born in a back-to-back house in Leeds?'

Holly wrote furiously. 'And on a personal level, Mr Mason, has your success in business been worth the price you've had to pay?' Holly noticed him flinch slightly before he answered this question with another one.

'What price do you mean?'

'Well, to put it another way, can you be a success in business and at the same time have a happy personal life?'

He paused. 'Of course you give a lot of energy to your work,' he conceded. He cleared his throat. 'Unfortunately, my own wife died twenty years ago, when my son was eight. Because of that I would say I'm not quite typical of businessmen who have to juggle home life and work. I never remarried.' Mr Mason stood up and looked out of his window at his wysteria, his rose garden, his Rolls Royce in the drive. 'But like other businessmen, I hope that much of my effort will benefit what's left of my family; my son, that is.' His voice was slower, less confident.

'Your son, Justin?' Holly prompted.

'Yes, Justin.' Mr Mason seemed absorbed by something in the garden.

'He'll inherit your newspapers?'

The old man nodded. 'The house, everything. In due course.'

'And there are no other children?'

He frowned. 'No.' He let the answer drift around the room. 'No, Justin will get everything. Provided he manages to stay in one piece.' It sounded sad, the way he said it, without hope or amusement.

'And is Justin interested in journalism too?' Holly went carefully, but not carefully enough.

The old man turned to face her. 'Your time's up, I'm afraid.' He looked at his watch. 'No more questions.' Back to the politician's smile. 'Well, Miss Adams, Miss Foster, Miss – er – Hayes, I hope you've got all the information you need. And now I have to go. I'll send Rachel to show you out. Very nice to meet you, and good luck with your assignment, yes!' He nodded at each of them, almost a small, formal bow, and he was gone.

'Ouch!' Tracy said very quietly.

'Not a happy man,' Belinda agreed.

Holly thought it was strange; you could have everything and still be unhappy. 'But Justin's in line to inherit every penny,' she said. 'So why on earth does he need thirty-five grand?'

'Cheer up. We knew the answer wouldn't just fall into our laps,' Belinda insisted. 'We're in here, that's the main thing, so now it's up to us!'

Rachel soon returned. She offered them cool drinks on the terrace. 'You've got quite a scoop,' she told them, 'and just before Mr Mason goes away. He has such a full schedule.'

Holly said it was all fascinating. 'I'd like to know more about the actual business side of things.' She looked eagerly at Rachel.

'Such as?'

'How the newspapers are put together, advertising, et cetera.'

'Our circulation figures. That sort of thing?'

'Yes. I'd be really grateful if you could spare me a few more minutes.' Holly didn't have to play-act her enthusiasm.

'Of course.' Ever obliging, Rachel Stone walked the girls out into the sunshine. The housekeeper brought out a tray of drinks. For a while Tracy and Belinda hung around while Holly asked questions.

'Say, would it be OK for us to check out the stables?' Tracy asked.

'Please!' Belinda added. Her face brightened immediately.

'Of course,' Rachel said again.

Tracy and Belinda left Holly to get on with the interview, while they wandered off to the stable yard.

'My friend loves horses,' Holly explained, as if it was some minor illness. 'I can't keep her away from them.'

'Which one?'

'Belinda. She's got her own thoroughbred, called Meltdown. She's mad about him.'

Rachel commiserated. 'Oh, I know, I always wanted a horse, didn't you?'

'No. I always wanted to be a reporter!' Holly confessed. 'I love everything to do with newspapers.'

'Yes, they're fascinating,' Rachel agreed.

Holly smiled. She and Rachel Stone were getting along fine.

6 One more false move

The stable was being mucked out by a boy with wavy brown hair. He looked the outdoor type in faded denims and a pale blue open-necked shirt. He introduced himself to Tracy and Belinda as Simon Clarke.

'Do you live here?' Tracy asked. Belinda was busy rubbing a horse's nose.

He nodded. 'My mother works for Mr Mason. She's the housekeeper.'

'What's it like?' Tracy let all her amazement about the place escape. 'I mean, it must be fabulous.'

Simon dug his fork into a pile of fresh hay. 'It's horrible, really,' he said. 'Like living in a museum,' he added grimly. He went off across the yard to connect a hosepipe to a water tap.

Belinda, not so wrapped up in the horses as she pretended, shot over to Tracy. 'I've just had a brilliant idea,' she said. 'This is what you do!'

'Me?'

'You. You chat him up. You wow him with your blonde good looks and toothpaste smile!'

'Simon? What for? I've already got a boyfriend!' Tracy was slow to follow Belinda's argument.

'No, stupid! If you chat him up, he'll fall in love with you and tell us everything we need to know!'

'About Justin?' Tracy looked doubtfully across at Simon in his denims and heavy black boots. She had to admit if it wasn't for Kurt, she might have shown some interest.

'Of course about Justin. That's why we're here, isn't it?' Belinda looked Tracy in the eye. 'We didn't get anywhere much with the old man himself, did we? He's much too clever to give away the family secrets.' Her gaze drifted across the yard. 'Whereas Simon . . .'

Tracy made a snap decision. 'OK,' she agreed with a shrug. 'All in the line of duty.'

Simon trailed the hose over to some empty water buckets, impatient to finish his work. 'Go and turn that tap on for us, will you,' he said to Tracy.

Tracy gave him a dazzling smile and did as she was told, treading daintily across the yard. Simon noticed her avoid the horse muck because of her fashion shoes. 'Not exactly dressed for it, is she?'

he muttered, glancing approvingly at Belinda's battered trainers. Belinda felt herself go red and refused to return Simon's smile.

When Tracy turned the tap on full blast, the water jet shot through the hose. The force of it snatched the nozzle out of Simon's hand. 'Watch out!' he yelled. Water sprayed everywhere, but mainly over Simon and Belinda.

Belinda shrieked. Tracy ran towards her. Simon swore and grabbed the hose. 'Go back!' he yelled at Tracy, 'Turn it down!'

Belinda sat in the hay, soaked to the skin. Simon joined her, and by the time Tracy turned down the tap and got back to them, they were both sitting there drenched, laughing their heads off.

Then Simon became very gallant. He helped Belinda up, took off her squelchy trainers and stood her in the sun to dry. 'Sorry,' he said over and over. But laughter kept bubbling up too. 'You don't half look funny!'

While he went off for dry clothes, Tracy came in with a quick change of plan. The blonde-haired, blue-eyed bit obviously hadn't worked. 'Right,' she said, with a healthy touch of malice, 'he may be able to resist my charms, but he's fallen for *you* all right.'

'No!' Belinda exclaimed. She was absolutely

hopeless with boys. She wished she could sink through the ground.

'Yes!' Tracy insisted sternly. 'So *you* can chat him up instead!'

Belinda's face was horror-struck. 'No!' she cried. 'Don't leave me!' She was still standing in the stable yard drying off. Suddenly she went from hot to cold and started to shiver.

Simon came back with a dry shirt. 'Here,' he said, smiling at her. 'You'd better have this.' And he went off to a discreet distance and pretended to be busy.

'Don't leave me!' Belinda pleaded again as she struggled into the dry shirt. 'Tracy, please don't go!' Simon was already returning, whistling loudly to let them know.

'*Well!*' Tracy was enjoying herself now. She spoke in a brisk, stagey voice. 'I'll just go and see how Holly's getting on. See you later, you two!' And she was gone. Belinda felt a terrible sensation of panic.

'Better?' Simon asked. He noticed Belinda was still shivering inside his shirt. 'Looks a lot nicer on you than it does on me,' he acknowledged. 'Fancy a coffee?'

Belinda groaned inwardly, but nodded anyway. Her loyalties were all over the place. True, she might get some useful information out of

65

Simon about Mr Mason and his son. But at what price? She'd have to put up with Simon obviously fancying her, a thing she detested. She hung on to her nerves and went in after him.

He took her into the workroom, full of tack, rope, a few tools and a kettle in one corner. To her surprise, it settled the butterflies in her stomach. She liked the smell of leather polish and the clutter everywhere. Soon she was relaxed. She even managed to smile.

'Do you really hate living here?' she asked, hands around a warm mug, curled up in a battered deck chair.

'Bits of it.' He still stared at her, then he took the plunge. 'Funny,' he said, 'some girls have all the frills, all the make-up. But you look good just natural!'

Belinda squirmed, swallowed, and tried to ignore him. 'Which bits don't you like?' she asked.

Simon shrugged. 'The place is OK, really, I suppose. The old man's all right.'

'But?'

'The son's a right idiot!' The words slipped out before he could stop them.

'Justin?' Belinda sat up in her chair. 'Why?'

'He thinks he's it, that's why. Lord of the Manor and all that. Do this, do that. He drives my mum mad. I just do my best to keep out of his way.'

'And do they get on, old Mr Mason and Justin?' Belinda had the scent of something important.

Simon snorted. 'You're joking! Justin's always arguing with him. "I want this, I want that." Just lately the old man's started to say no!'

Belinda nodded. 'They have rows about money?' She almost didn't mind when Simon came up to the chair, leant along the back of it and put his hand on her shoulder. 'Is that it?'

'Well, he spends it like water, so what does he expect? He's always off clubbing, gambling on the horses, whatever. And it's not even his to spend. He never did a day's work. Anyway, the old man's sick of it.'

'So what's he done?'

But Simon hadn't finished. 'Besides, he has all these women.'

'Girlfriends?'

'A different one every week, it seems. The old man's a bit old-fashioned about that too. Some of them are married, I reckon. He can't stand that, won't have them in the house, so Justin has to sneak them in. Old Mr Mason's dead straight about things like that.'

'What's Justin say?'

'Nothing. Just sulks. He does it behind the old man's back, like I say.' Simon drank his coffee thoughtfully. 'Serves him right.'

'What does? Who?' Belinda was trying to keep up and memorise this all at once.

'Justin. Serves him right. The old man found out about the gambling debts and a scandal with some married woman.'

'Small, pretty, with long red hair?' Belinda put in an inspired guess.

Simon nodded. 'How do you know?'

'Never mind. What happened then?'

Simon smiled slowly. 'The old man stopped his allowance. Just like that. Cut off the money, said without it the women wouldn't give Justin the time of day. The money was all they were after! Justin went mad.'

'I bet he did. When did all this happen?' Belinda's mind worked quickly over the information.

'About a month ago.'

'So he'd got no money. Then to make matters worse he went and crashed his car? It was in the papers,' she reminded him.

Simon grinned again. 'According to him. I must say I thought he'd done it on purpose for the insurance money.'

Belinda nearly dropped her mug of coffee. Her

68

mouth fell open. 'You mean, he faked the crash?' She tried to sound naive and shocked.

'That's what I thought straight off at the time. Well if he did, it backfired on him. Oh, he managed to convince the police and everyone that it was genuine, with the help of a tame GP. All that about losing his memory! He put in his insurance claim, all hunky-dory!'

'But?' Belinda almost didn't want to hear the next bit.

'But old Mr Mason probably cottoned on too. So he goes up to Justin face to face and tells him he's got to get another car exactly the same to replace the one he's smashed up. He's not to keep the cash, see! My mum says Justin's face fell a mile. Serves him right!'

Belinda sat and thought. All that planning for nothing. 'Poor Justin,' she said, shaking her head.

'Poor Justin, my foot! Anyway, the old man's told him if he makes one more false move, any more gambling, any more women, and he'll cut him off for good without another penny!'

'He'll disinherit him?' This time Belinda's surprise was genuine. 'Wow!' No wonder Mr Mason had been too sensitive to answer Holly's questions about Justin.

'He has to be a good boy from now on.' Simon

smiled. 'You know what, I'm enjoying telling you all this!'

Pleased with what she'd found out, Belinda smiled back. 'Simon, thank you!' She sprang up, but fought off the urge to hug him, in case he got the wrong impression.

Simon went red. 'What for? I just drenched you to the skin!'

'I know. Listen, can I keep this shirt for a bit? I have something to do after I've found the others.'

Seeing an opportunity slipping away, Simon took the plunge. 'Will you go out with me then?' He didn't have time to put it any better than that.

Belinda couldn't believe her ears. She'd never been on a date before, and she didn't want to start now. But they couldn't afford to lose Simon from the picture. 'OK,' she found herself saying. 'When?' She was going to *kill* Tracy!

'Tomorrow. At the ice rink. Seven o'clock?'

'F-fine!' Terror made her stutter. Could this really be happening? She'd said yes to a *skating date*? She hated ice-skating! 'See you then!'

And before Simon could lean forward to kiss her, Belinda dashed off to find Tracy. She didn't want to forget the least little scrap of what Simon had told her!

* * *

Tracy was on the terrace, looking worried and shaken. 'I've just seen him!' she whispered.

'Who? Justin Mason?' Belinda steadied her.

Tracy nodded. 'I came back over here to find Holly and Rachel, but they'd gone off some place. I peeped in there to see if they were in the old man's office, but it was Justin I saw.'

'And? Did he see you?'

'No. He was checking the desk diary. He looked serious. It was scary. Then he left the room and I nipped in through these French window things to look at the diary too.'

Belinda raised her eyebrows. 'That took some nerve. So, what was in there?'

Tracy took a breath. 'So, he'd been looking up his father's appointments. And you know, Holly's name and telephone number are written down there large as life, with our school and everything. He's seen it! He knows who she is!'

Belinda nodded. This was serious. 'And where is he now?'

'Who knows? Hanging around somewhere, spying.'

'We'd best get Holly out of here,' Belinda decided. 'In case he tries something nasty.'

'You think he'll stop her poking around?'

'I would, wouldn't you? From what I hear, his

whole life's a mess.' Quickly she filled Tracy in on the facts. 'The last thing he wants is anyone poking around investigating the car crash.'

'What do you think he'd do?'

Belinda shook her head. But Tracy's imagination was as vivid as hers. 'Yeah,' she agreed. 'We'd better get her out of here!'

They decided to go straight round to the front of the house. They would knock and ask where Holly was; nothing subtle.

Rachel Stone answered the door, fresh and smiling. 'Hello, you two,' she said. 'You've lost Holly?'

They nodded.

'She's a very thorough young lady, your Holly Adams. I'm most impressed!'

They nodded again. 'Where is she?'

'Well, she wanted to find out more about running a grand house like this. Once she'd finished with the business side, that is. So she's interviewing Mrs Clarke, the housekeeper.'

'Oh, no!' they groaned silently. How long would that take?

Round every corner, lurking in every shadow they felt the tall thin shadow of Justin Mason.

7 *A secret affair*

Mrs Clarke had a flat on the top floor of the house. It was cosy and pretty, with pale blue wallpaper and sloping ceilings. She was a friendly, easy-going woman, ready to help with their interview. But there were some things she wouldn't talk about, she warned: 'Personal details about Mr Mason and such like. I wouldn't want to mention personal details.' She recalled all the newspaper scandals about the royals, where ladies-in-waiting sold their stories for thousands of pounds. Mrs Clarke had more self-respect, she told Holly.

'Of course!' Holly smiled. 'I wouldn't expect you to do that. That wouldn't be right!' She got out the Mystery Club's notebook and looked professional.

'Not that I couldn't tell you things that would make your hair curl,' the housekeeper said, settling herself into an armchair. 'I've never been interviewed before. I think I might quite like it!' She smiled good-humouredly.

'Now, how much entertaining does a successful man like Mr Mason have to do?' Holly asked briskly. She had a feeling that Mrs Clarke wouldn't be a hard nut to crack.

'Lots. He might have people to dinner here about twice a week. Dinner parties for up to twelve guests. I do all the cooking. Miss Stone comes and discusses the menu with me first of all, then it's up to me to organise everything: cooking, employing extra staff and so on.'

'That must be very hard work,' Holly said sympathetically.

'Oh, it is, and Mr Mason always says a special thank-you. Old Mr Mason that is.'

Holly saw Mrs Clarke cross and uncross her legs. She saw her shake her head and lose a little battle with herself to stay loyal to the Masons. There was no need even to ask the questions, Holly realised; Mrs Clarke was set in for a good gossip.

Holly smiled, nodded and jotted things down.

'Not like young Mr Mason, mind you. You can do things for him until you're blue in the face, and all you get is insults and more orders. He's never heard of the word thank-you!'

For a second conscience struck at Mrs Clarke. 'See, it's not Mr Mason I'm complaining about, is it? He pays my wages and he's a good employer.

But that son of his shouldn't be allowed.' She shook her neatly permed head. 'Well, it's not fair on the old man. I'm always saying that to Miss Stone, when I find something's missing from a shelf or a bookcase. I say to her it shouldn't be allowed.' Mrs Clarke leaned forward. 'We both know who's taken it. He sells it to one of those friends of his who call themselves antique dealers. I call them thieves! Justin invites them over here when Mr Mason's away. They sit up drinking till all hours. Anyway, I tell Miss Stone it's not fair on the old man!' Her fair skin went red with indignation.

'What does Miss Stone say?'

'She says, what can we do? The old man knows these things go missing. It was an old piece of pewter last time. You know, one of those huge, really old plates above the fireplace down in the hall. He knows what his son gets up to. He does nothing about it; that's what I can't understand. If it was my Simon . . .' She leaned further forward and paused for breath. 'You see, Miss Stone doesn't like to upset the old man. She's very fond of him!' She raised her eyebrows. '*Very* fond!'

Holly started as a new picture clicked into place. 'You mean . . .'

'I'm not saying anything! I'm just telling you

Miss Stone is very fond of old Mr Mason.'
Mrs Clarke pulled her lips tight. 'And I'm
very fond of Miss Stone, see. So I'm saying
nothing!

'You mean . . .' Holly was dazed.

'I'm only saying that no one else would put up
with that obnoxious Justin always criticising and
name calling. Not unless they were very fond of
the old man!'

'But she's his secretary!' Holly repeated. *And
she's half his age*, she thought.

'Secretary, girl Friday, whatever they're called
these days. She looks after him better than you
could imagine. She worships him!' Mrs Clarke
sat and nodded knowingly. 'She's a lovely girl,
and I'm not saying a word against her! Anyway,
who could blame her? Mr Mason's been alone
all these years. It's time he got married again!'

'Yes, but . . .' Holly was trying very hard to
make sense of things. Mrs Clarke was actually
telling her that old Mr Mason and Rachel were
secretly in love!

'Nothing nasty or cheap,' Mrs Clarke assured
her. 'She's much too nice a girl!'

'But how do you know?' Holly wanted to
check the evidence.

'Ah!' Mrs Clarke leaned back, and then forwards again. She took another deep breath.

'Holly!' It was Tracy's voice calling out from down the corridor. She sounded worried.

Mrs Clarke jumped as if she'd been shot.

'It's OK, it's just my friend,' Holly said. But by now the mood was broken. Rachel knocked and came in, with Tracy and Belinda following. Mrs Clarke gave Holly a warning look and stood up to meet them.

'Tracy and Belinda were worried that you might have forgotten the time.' Rachel came in smiling, unsuspecting. 'And I wanted to remind Margaret that the Hoover repair man is due any minute. So,' she beamed at Holly, 'have you found out everything you needed to know?'

'Y – yes, thanks.' Holly felt her face colour up. She didn't dare look at the housekeeper.

'In fact, here's the man coming down the drive now,' Rachel said, looking out the window. 'Would you three mind very much if Margaret and I just pop down to sort him out? I won't be long.' Brisk as ever, she was gone. Mrs Clarke followed more slowly.

The Mystery Club was left alone in the high attic flat. Holly leaned back against a wall. 'I just don't believe it!'

'What?'

'What don't you believe?'

'*Shh!*' Holly had to pinch herself to see if this

crazy news was part of a dream. 'Rachel's having an affair with Mr Mason!'

Belinda gasped.

'Wow!' cried Tracy. 'That means they'll get married. Then they'll have loads of babies and Justin won't be in line for any of this!' She spread her arms as her imagination raced on.

'*Shh!*' Holly said again. She could hear footsteps coming up the stairs.

'I don't believe it,' Belinda said. 'I don't think the old man would do that. He wouldn't have a secret affair, would he?' She recalled his absolutely correct manner, his belief in hard work. 'It doesn't fit!'

'Belinda!' Tracy whispered. 'Trust you! Of course it fits. Everyone does it these days. Every old millionaire trades in his wife for a younger model, and Mr Mason doesn't even have an old one to trade in!'

Belinda still shook her head. 'Not this old millionaire!'

'Shh, you two!' Holly strained to listen. 'Those aren't Rachel's footsteps!' They were too heavy and cautious.

The footsteps paused on the top step. Holly looked at Belinda and Tracy. 'Let's go. Come on, we've got to get out of here!'

They fled from the housekeeper's room, along

the corridor away from the heavy footsteps. They ran single file down the length of the house. Then they turned to see the silent figure of Justin Mason. He stood by Mrs Clarke's door and watched the girls disappear down the back staircase.

They ran, hearts spinning with fear. They scrambled down two flights of stairs into the back kitchen. 'This way!' Holly said, recognising the oak beams of the entrance hall. They ran by the old fireplace gleaming with pewter and coats of arms, across the flagged floor.

But still Justin Mason was there in the driveway before them. He stood in their path, flanked by the Great Danes. He stood in the sun dressed completely in black, legs wide apart, grinning. Then he ordered the dogs forward.

They sprang; heavy, deep-snarling, ferocious, huge creatures. Holly, Belinda and Tracy scattered across the front lawn, over the flower-beds. The hot breath of the dogs covered their legs as they scaled the wall. They heard their wild snarling, and above it, as they jumped to safety, the wilder sound of Justin's unrestrained laughter.

8 A simple mistake

'Right, so we have the motive!' Holly declared. They'd taken refuge in Meltdown's stable behind Belinda's house, where it was quiet and peaceful. They still felt shaken, although the dogs hadn't pursued them beyond the Manor House walls. 'The perfect motive, and one we'd never have guessed!'

'He's short of cash,' Belinda said bluntly.

'He has a cash-flow problem, as my mother would say!' said Holly.

'He also has a personality problem!' Tracy put in, recalling his cruel laughter. She shuddered.

'Besides which, the fake crash hasn't solved things for him.' Belinda absent-mindedly fed Meltdown a handful of hay. 'All the insurance money will have to go on another car to replace the one he crashed.'

'Poor thing!' Tracy mocked.

'Unless he can manage to get it cheaper some-how?' Holly wondered aloud.

The others shook their heads. 'How?'

Holly shrugged. 'OK, what else do we have?'

'Bruises!' Belinda complained. She'd knocked her shins on the wall as they'd scrambled over.

'A *boyfriend*!' Tracy said, pretending to swoon. 'A hunk. A horsey hunk who's head over heels in love with Belinda!' She gave Holly all the details. 'And what's more, they've got a date tomorrow night at the ice rink!' She fluttered her eyelashes and sighed.

Belinda swiped her with a knot of hay. 'Who says I'm going to meet him, anyway?' It had been a rash moment when she'd said yes to Simon.

'Listen,' Holly said, 'we'd best write some of this down.' She pulled out the Mystery Club's red notebook and began to make case notes. 'Since we're talking about romance, what about this one between Rachel and Mr Mason?'

The other two considered. 'I think yes,' Tracy said. 'Because you say Mrs Clarke seems a pretty reliable type, OK? Sure, she talks a lot, but she tells the truth as far as we know. And she gets a pretty close look at what goes on up at the Manor House!'

'But he's so old!' Belinda objected.

'And so rich!' Tracy reminded her. 'Anyhow, one thing's for sure, Justin's pretty ruthless when it comes to dealing with problems, and we're one of them. In fact, now I reckon we're top of his list!'

'We've got to be careful,' Holly agreed.

They were silent then, listening only to Holly's pen on the page, and to the slight shifting of Meltdown's hooves against the stall.

'What time is it?' Holly suddenly broke in. 'Is it lunch-time?'

Belinda nodded. 'It's just after one o'clock.'

'I told my mum I'd be home for the builders' merchant,' Holly said in a rush. 'He's delivering some stone. I'd better go!' She scrambled out of the stable, grabbed her bike and pedalled off. 'I'll ring you tonight!' she yelled, before the others could catch their breaths.

Belinda and Tracy stood and watched her fly off down the hill.

Holly made it back home just in time. She'd left the message with the man at the builders' yard that she'd be back at one thirty in time for the lorry to deliver its load. She raced up their lane just in time to see it arrive at the gate. The driver had jumped out of his cab to peer into the empty yard. Holly came up behind him, breathless.

'Sorry I'm late,' she said. She dumped her bike and went up to him.

'Adams?' the man said roughly, referring to an invoice in his hand.

'Yes.' She nodded.

'Your mum in?'

'No, but it's OK. I know all about this. It's a load of extra stone for the extension, see? We need it dumping over here.' She opened the gate wide for his tip-up truck and pointed to a space over by the garage door.

'You the daughter?' the man asked. He didn't look at her, so this wasn't a chat-up. He seemed keen to sort out exactly what was going on. He was stocky and balding. Too old, Holly thought, for the heavy metal death's head design on his black T-shirt, and he needed a shave. There was a faded tattoo on his right arm.

'Yes, I'm Holly Adams. My mum's told me what to do; it's OK!' She didn't like it when adults did this to her. After all, she wasn't a little kid.

'Anyone else at home?' The man looked around, up at the cottage windows, back down the lane.

Holly noticed that all the other workmen's vans had gone from the yard. 'Everyone's off on their lunch break, I expect. You'll just have to believe I know what I'm doing!' She was getting really fed up. She hoped she hadn't pedalled all the way over here for nothing.

The man nodded slowly.

'Unless you want me to ring my mother at work so you can check everything with her?' Holly said sarcastically.

The man started backwards, shook his head and took a swift look at Holly. 'No problem,' he said. He hauled himself back up into the cab. 'Best get on with it.'

She began gradually and carefully to wave the truck in through the wide gate. The driver leaned out sideways, then pointed at the garage door. 'You'll have to stand right there. Keep waving me across,' he said with a jerk of his thumb. 'I can't see much from in here!'

Holly nodded impatiently. She stood over by the white door of their garage, waving and shouting, 'Further, a bit more, yes, further!' The truck manoeuvred towards her, load first. 'Stop!' she shouted, putting up her hand to catch the driver's attention.

But the driver didn't stop. The truck engine drowned Holly's words, as the giant wheels picked up speed. The load of stone swayed and slid backwards against the closed tailgate.

'Stop!' Holly screamed. She flattened herself against the garage door. The truck kept on coming. Exhaust fumes choked her. The engine roared. 'Stop, *stop*!' she cried.

She had time, a split-second, to think, *This is it!* But she was frozen, paralysed by the monster bearing down on her. She felt the garage door shudder; she felt the hot exhaust belching all over her. In seconds she would be crushed to death. She closed her eyes in terror.

Then, miraculously, the door lifted up inch by inch and someone was screaming, 'In here, Holly! Quick, in here!'

It was Jamie. He lifted the door and grabbed her legs. Holly ducked, and rolled through the gap, into the darkness of the garage. She heard the harsh crunch of metal as the truck hit the half-open door, hissed, then ground to a halt. Holly lay there, eyes closed, listening to the crumpling metal.

Then Jamie started yelling again. He ran out into the yard. 'Hey, stop!' But the engine roared again, and the truck lurched forward, the driver ignoring his shout.

Instead, he shot the monster vehicle straight across the yard, racing first gear. In an instant he was out through the gate, driving like a madman, like a hit and run vandal. Out into the lane, raising dust, mounting grass verges, the truck, still loaded with stone, careered off out of sight.

Holly pulled herself into a ball on the floor of the garage and waited for the shuddering to stop.

'Wake up!' Jamie ran back and crouched over her. 'Holly, wake up!'

'It's OK, look, she's breathing!' There was another voice, another face. Holly felt the dust clear and the daylight filter through. She smelt the oil of the garage floor. As she opened her eyes, she saw Jamie bending over her with his friend Richard.

Holly had never been so happy to see her little brother. Once in a while, Jamie came through!

'He did that on purpose!' Richard kept saying after they'd all made their way into the kitchen. Holly was scrubbing the oil marks off her face and hands. 'We saw him through the window. He did it on purpose!'

Jamie stared at Holly and nodded. 'He put his foot down on the accelerator, just when you'd told him to stop!'

Holly shook her head. The shock had robbed her of her tongue. At last, as she scrubbed the last marks off her cheek, she was able to speak. 'Maybe he didn't hear me yell at him to stop.' It was what she wanted to believe.

The boys raised their voices. 'No, he did it on purpose!' Richard insisted. He was a serious boy, not given to flights of imagination. 'Honest!'

'He must have been drunk then,' she said. But Holly could remember how he'd checked all the details on the invoice, holding it in a steady hand. 'No,' she said.

'Let's ring the police!' Jamie grabbed for the phone. 'He just tried to run you over!'

'No.' Holly stopped him. 'We've got to think. Why on earth would he want to do that?'

The boys, round-eyed with excitement, could offer no reasons. Why should a man in a lorry who she'd never seen before want to run her over? It was crazy. Totally frightening and crazy!

'Hang on a sec, I've seen him before!' Jamie said, thunderstruck. 'I've just remembered where I saw that skull thing on his T-shirt!'

'Where, Jamie?' Holly urged. 'Where did you see him?'

'This morning. In town. Before Richard and I came up home. We got fish and chips opposite the Crown.'

'No, that wasn't him,' Richard cut in. 'The chip shop man was much older . . .'

'Not him, stupid! I'm talking about the one

outside the pub, with the T-shirt with that skull thing on the front. That's why I remember!'

'What was he doing?' Holly asked. She could tell when her brother was telling the truth. 'Go on, Jamie, tell me!'

Jamie caught his breath. 'Let's just think. He was standing there talking to someone, a big, loud talk, a sort of argument.'

'Who, the truck driver and someone else? What was the other person like?'

'Tall. He'd got dark hair. I think his clothes were all black as well. Yes, definitely!'

Holly's heart did the familiar somersault. She grabbed yesterday's newspaper from the pile by the TV and showed Jamie the crash photo and the picture of the driver below. 'Him? Was it him?' She jabbed a finger down on to the page.

'That's him!' Jamie cried. He read the name: 'Justin Mason!'

She sat down, nodding her head like a puppet. In her bones she knew this was true. Justin Mason had planned it. God knows how he'd set it up, or who the truck driver was, or how much he'd had to pay him. But the truth drilled into her brain as she sat there in their half-finished kitchen.

'Hi there!' came a man's voice behind her.

Holly, her nerves still in shreds, jumped with fright.

It was the builder, wandering back from his lunch break.

'No stone been delivered yet?' he asked, strolling in behind.

Holly and the boys just stared stupidly at him.

'I'd better get on the phone to that builders' yard,' he decided.

They heard him pick up the phone in the hallway and tell them off. 'You know that load of stone I ordered? Well, see if you can get it up here double quick. We're stuck without it.' He paused, then raised his voice again. 'Don't be stupid, of course your bloke hasn't been up here with the truck yet! I wouldn't be ringing you if he had, would I?'

They heard the builder slam down the phone, and followed him out to the sound of a truck returning. The four of them stood there in the yard as the lorry came back to deliver its load. Holly could feel herself start to shake again, but this time a different driver jumped down from the cab.

'What kept you?' the builder asked. 'I've just been on the blower to your boss!'

The young, fair-haired driver rolled up the

sleeves of his checked shirt and shrugged. 'Thirsty work,' he said. 'I just stopped off for a quick one at the Crown. Low alcohol, mind you!'

The builder nodded knowingly.

'Then a mate of mine comes in, says he'll run the whole load up here for me if I like, for the price of a pint when he gets back. Never look a gift horse in the mouth, I say. So I says, yes, go ahead. But he's back in half an hour and he's made a right pig's ear of the job. Tells me he's found the place all right, but there's no one around and he's backed the whole lot into the garage door! I ask you. Says he panics and drives straight back out of the yard with the load still on!'

The two men strolled over to look at the damage to the garage door, arguing about who should pay to put it right.

For a moment Holly thought again. Yes that was it, a simple mistake and a sudden panic. The man had bungled a favour for his mate. The truth was too horrible.

But she saw Jamie and Richard shake their heads. They'd seen the driver arguing with Justin Mason. And she remembered the death's head on the heavy metal T-shirt, the mechanical look on the face of the man as he began to reverse the truck. She remembered the deliberate roar of the engine as the truck bore down on her.

It was planned. It was deliberate. Justin Mason had told him to do it. Justin Mason had just tried to kill her!

9 Another close call

'What happened to the garage door?' Mr Adams asked next morning. It had been dark when he'd arrived back home.

'A truck bashed into it.' Holly kept her voice matter of fact and casual. She shot a warning look at Jamie, who was crunching his cornflakes.

She knew it was better to keep the truth a secret. On the one hand, her parents might not believe her. On the other, if they did, they might stop her from ever going anywhere by herself again.

Mrs Adams came downstairs, organised for work as usual. 'It's OK, they say they'll fix it,' she told her husband. 'They were full of apologies about it.'

'Who's paying?'

'The driver from the builders' merchant. He knows a man who can fix it. A very nice man!'

'That's OK then.' Mr Adams disappeared behind his newspaper.

'. . . And that's how an attempted murder got hushed up!' Holly told Tracy and Belinda later. They were on their way to the ice rink to meet up with Simon.

'And the mystery deepens!' Belinda said. They were in town, waiting for the controlled crossing to turn green. 'Who's this homicidal truck driver then? Where did he spring from?'

'One of Justin Mason's disreputable friends, probably. He's in with a bad crowd, according to Simon's mum,' Holly reminded them. 'Maybe the truck driver's one of them.'

'Ouch!' Mention of Simon sent Belinda off course. The green man flashed at last and she developed a limp as they all hurried across the road. 'I think I've sprained my ankle!' she moaned. She brightened. 'Now I won't be able to go ice-skating!' She hobbled melodramatically across the road. 'Tell Simon I couldn't make it!' she moaned.

'No way!' Tracy pulled her up on the kerb at the far side. 'Come on, or we'll be late.' She'd arranged to meet up with Kurt at the bus stop.

'Listen!' Belinda's panic grew as they sat on the top deck a few minutes later, heading out of town. She turned from Tracy, who was busy filling Kurt in on who Simon was, to Holly. 'Do you think we're doing the right thing here? I mean, should you be out in public, after what they tried to do to you yesterday? Maybe we should just go right back home and have a quiet night in watching a video or something?'

Holly shook her head. Belinda was right about the possible dangers, but her motives were all wrong. 'No, we're going ice-skating!' she said. 'Simon won't bite, you know!'

'I know he won't bite.' Belinda looked miserable as she sat in silence until they reached the stop on the outskirts of town. The ice rink was visible as they got off. 'But I can't even ice-skate!' she wailed.

The others ignored her.

The rink flashed out a welcome from across the main road, neon signs glowing in the gathering dusk. A crowd of kids lingered in the entrance, making their way up an open stairway along the glass front of the building.

'Wait!' Kurt warned. The traffic was heavy and fast.

Just then a low, black monster of a car sped past, unmistakeable. Holly stepped quickly back on to the pavement, caught hold of her panic,

94

and made a grab for Belinda. 'That was him!' she gasped.

'Who?'

'Justin Mason!' The car's red brake lights flashed at the bend then vanished.

'Are you sure?'

'Yes, in his new car. I saw him, with his girlfriend!'

'Did he see you?'

Holly nodded. 'I think so. But, listen, there was someone else in there with them, sitting in the back seat!'

'OK, let's cross,' Tracy said. She was still in the dark about what they were getting excited about. 'Come on, what are we waiting for?'

It wasn't until they were in the foyer of the ice rink, joining the crowd, that Holly could take Belinda and Tracy to one side. 'It was the maniac truck driver!' she said. 'In the back seat. All dressed up in a suit like some night-club bouncer. But it was him all right!'

'Let's just check some of this out.' Tracy had spotted Simon waiting nervously a couple of steps up the wide metal stairway. Like Belinda, he seemed to live in one set of clothes; still the denims and the pale blue shirt, so he was easy to recognise. 'There's your horsey hunk now!' she whispered as Belinda shrank back.

'Hi!' Tracy called, completely confident. Belinda checked her sweaty palms.

'Hi, Simon. Simon, this is Kurt. Kurt, Simon.' Tracy raced through the formalities. 'Listen, Simon, did Justin Mason get his new car yet?' She put an arm through his to lead him up to the rink.

'Hang on.' Simon turned and looked for Belinda.

'Did he?' Tracy pestered.

'As a matter of fact, yes, earlier today. Listen, it wasn't you I asked out, was it?' he said touchily.

Tracy ignored him and yelled down at the others, 'He did! Justin took delivery of his car today!'

They all bunched together in the queue for skates. 'That was quick, wasn't it?' Holly asked. 'So who delivered the car?'

'I dunno. Just some bloke. He brought it up to the house this afternoon.' Simon was edging closer to Belinda in the queue. 'Some friend of Justin's, I think.'

'Dark-skinned, going bald, with a tattoo here on his right arm?' As usual Holly followed a hunch. Her pulse raced as she waited for the answer.

'That sounds like him,' Simon said. He smiled

awkwardly at Belinda. 'Why all this interest in Justin's new car?'

'We just saw him drive by, that's all,' Belinda reassured him.

Soon they each clutched a pair of ice skates and headed together for the vast rink.

Tracy and Kurt put on their skates and glided off like professionals, in and out of the flow. Holly followed them. She settled into the rhythm and speed of skating, ready for a good think. Where did Justin's sinister friend – the maniac truck driver, alias car salesman, alias night-clubbing companion – fit in? Oddly, she felt safer speeding along on a pair of steel blades than she had done for days. She was safe in a crowd.

Meanwhile, Belinda was clinging to the side barrier for dear life.

'I – I've never been ice-skating before!' she confessed to Simon. Bodies flashed by, doing pirouettes and triple axles. Tiny kids speed-skated around the rink.

'It's easy,' he said. 'Nothing to it. Look.' He took three or four confident steps ahead. 'Come on!'

She took three or four terrified steps, tottered and collapsed in his arms. 'Sorry!'

'Don't be!' A huge grin split his face. Clearly

this was his idea of heaven. He gently stood Belinda on her feet. 'Try again.'

She tried, tottered and collapsed on Simon for twenty whole minutes. Kurt and Tracy flashed by like Olympic gold medallists, arms entwined. Holly kept up her steady, thoughtful pace. Cold all over, dodging the blades, Belinda came up for air.

Simon helped her. 'You're improving!' he encouraged. 'Too bad!'

'What do you mean?' Suddenly she realised how much physical contact she'd been allowing. 'Break time!' she declared. She went down on all fours and crawled decisively off the ice.

'Pity,' Simon said, shaking his head. They took off their skates and headed for the café.

'Not at all!' Belinda argued firmly.

'But I was enjoying that!'

'Tough.' She sat down opposite him at the table. 'Anyway, you can make yourself useful and tell me all you know about your employer's son. Dish the dirt; go on!'

'Why all the interest?'

'Natural curiosity,' she said, eyes sparkling. If she was able to get more information from Simon, the torture of having a temporary boy-friend might just be worthwhile.

'There's plenty of it to dish,' he warned. 'And

I'm not the one to stick up for Justin, as you know!'

'I know. So go on! Tell me what's been going on at the Manor House today,' Belinda said. 'Is Justin pleased with his new car?'

'It's a miracle!' Simon mocked. 'Just as if the crash had never happened. Same colour, same year, same wheel trims, and ten thousand miles less on the clock!'

'Is Mr Mason happy about it?' Belinda stared down from the café window at the skaters gliding soundlessly below.

'He's still away in London.'

'How come this car appeared so quick?' Belinda asked.

Simon shrugged. 'A friend of a friend. I don't know. Sometimes Justin knows how to pull strings.' Simon frowned across at her. 'I can just remember that smug swine's face as that mate of his handed over the new car keys, like he'd won the football pools! It doesn't make him any nicer to know, I can tell you!'

'Has he been treating you badly then?' Belinda succeeded in sounding sympathetic as well as curious.

'Not me especially. But he's been picking on Rachel, on Miss Stone. He does that when the old man's away.'

'What does he do?' Belinda's surprise was genuine.

'Pushes her around. Asks for cash. Gets nasty when she says no.'

'Does she say no, then?'

'Sometimes. She looks after all the household money; wages and everything. So she has to keep everything straight for the old man.'

'What does Justin do?'

'Locks her up in the office. Starts shouting. Dunno. I can't hear, the walls are too thick.' He paused for breath. 'It just sickens me to know that Rachel sometimes hands over her own money, just to keep Justin quiet!'

'Like today?' Belinda pictured the slight figure of Rachel Stone being backed into a corner by tall, mean Justin. Her blood boiled.

'Yeah, a big row today,' Simon continued. Together they stared down at the mesmerising pattern of skaters on the ice. 'That Tracy can skate a bit, I'll say that,' Simon admitted, distracted for a moment.

'That sounds like a compliment!' They went up to the glass partition for a better view. 'Where's Holly? I haven't spotted her,' Belinda said. She searched in vain for a girl in a white top and black trousers.

'There!' Simon pointed out. Holly was swooping round the outside of knots of skaters. She seemed not to see two boys cut across the middle of the ice, against the flow, making straight for her.

'Holly, watch out!' Belinda yelled, hammering on the glass. Holly didn't look up. The two youths headed her off in a pincer movement, while Belinda and Simon stood there helpless.

But Tracy had spotted them. She shot like an arrow into the outside lane, caught Holly by the arm and swung her off course. The two boys, heads down, missed their mark. They met empty space, then each other. They clashed shoulders, their skates sliced the ice, then their heads crashed against the barrier. Meanwhile, Tracy steered her friend to safety.

'You OK?' Tracy asked. Kurt had stayed to watch the two dazed youths pick themselves up. Others came and jeered. A crowd gathered until an attendant came along and cleared the area. Scowling and bruised, the pair melted into the dark outer rim of the rink.

Holly nodded that she was fine. 'A close thing though,' she admitted. 'Who were those idiots?'

Tracy shook her head quickly. 'I don't know.'

'Tracy, you don't think . . .' Holly put two and

two together. Another narrow escape, another piece of bad luck, or Justin Mason and his friends on her trail again?

'No!' Tracy tried to sound confident. 'It was an accident!'

Holly blew a cloud of steam into the cold air. 'You don't think maybe . . .' She couldn't ignore the possibility that once again, Justin was after her.

Tracy shook her head, refusing to hear another word. 'Let's not get paranoid.' She led Holly off the ice.

By this time Belinda and Simon had hurried down from the café to meet them. 'Did you see those two gorillas?' Simon blurted out. 'Boy, did they have it in for you!'

The three girls looked at one another in silence. If it was true, and Justin was still trying to scare them off, he was certainly succeeding!

10 Asking for trouble

'If you ask me, you lot are just asking for trouble!' Simon delivered his verdict as they cycled together through the park. They were on their way to watch Kurt play cricket, and Simon had tagged along at Kurt's invitation. It was Sunday and the park was full of day-trippers.

'We didn't ask you!' Tracy swerved around a shaggy cairn terrier which yapped at her front wheel.

Belinda tried a more tactful line. 'You've got to understand,' she told him. 'We don't look for trouble, it just finds us. Or rather, it finds Holly.'

'OK, then,' Simon acknowledged. 'But why not let the whole thing rest now? I mean, you've proved your point. Justin's a big crook, and you're not telling me anything I didn't know already. Yes, he's perfectly capable of robbing people blind. Yes, he probably crashed his car deliberately. He probably even hired people and

103

sent them out to get Holly. I wouldn't put it past him. But why not let it drop now?'

The girls screeched to a halt on the crest of the old stone footbridge. They turned to stare at Simon, wide-eyed.

'Let it drop!' they echoed.

'Because we haven't solved the mystery yet,' Holly said, matter of factly. 'We don't know *why* he's doing it. That's the whole point.'

They pedalled on towards the cricket pitch. The sun shone, there was the sound of leather against wood and the smell of tea brewing in the pavilion. On a day like this, Willow Dale was paradise.

Even Tracy understood the attractions of the game: the smooth green pitch, the purple moor as a backdrop, and Kurt standing there in cricket whites, tall and upright.

'Hi!' she called, giving him a big wave. He responded with a business-like smile before crouching close to the wicket with his hands cupped, ready.

Simon waited for the girls to lean their bikes against the fence. They all settled down to watch the game. In his way he was as stubborn as they were. 'I'm only telling you for your own good, you know.'

'Thanks, but we can look after ourselves.'

Holly settled, cross-legged, on the grass. Belinda gave him a grateful smile. Tracy tossed her blonde head.

'But it's dangerous to carry on!' Simon warned. He seemed genuinely worried about them all.

'We know!' they said.

'No, you don't. You don't know Justin!'

A sprinkle of polite applause interrupted them. Kurt had caught someone out. Tracy jumped up and gave a wild cheer. Everyone around her stared disapprovingly. 'Oops!' she said, blushing as she dropped back down on to the grass. She'd never understand the silence at cricket matches.

'Hey,' she said, stretching out full length, 'I just had an idea!' She turned her head towards Simon.

Simon groaned.

'You could ask Rachel to help us!'

'What?'

'Yes!' Holly and Belinda agreed.

'No! I can't believe what I'm hearing!'

'Oh, yes,' Belinda coaxed. 'Rachel is the real key to this. I'm sure of it!'

But Simon refused to change his mind. 'It's too dangerous,' was all he said. And no amount of pleading looks would shift him.

When the cricket stopped for tea and Simon

went off to talk to Kurt, the Mystery Club drew together in a huddle.

'You're right,' Holly told Belinda. 'I think Rachel does hold all the answers.'

'But Simon won't help us.' Belinda glanced helplessly across at him.

Holly smiled. 'He means well.'

'He's in love!' Tracy sighed sarcastically. 'He wants to protect you. It's sweet!'

Belinda shuddered and shot Tracy a withering look.

'I still think,' Holly said slowly, 'that Rachel would be on our side.'

'Sure,' Tracy agreed. 'It's obvious what she has to gain if we can expose Justin. Once he's out of the way, she can go right ahead and marry Old Man Mason with no one to stop her! From her point of view, prison would be the perfect place for Justin!'

Belinda agreed. 'No more problems with hanging on to the family pewter. No more bullying. What could she possibly have to lose?'

'Besides, she liked me,' Holly grinned. 'We really hit if off!'

It was easy to convince themselves that Rachel Stone would help. They would have to ask her, with or without Simon's help.

They sat and watched the cricketers stroll back

on. Kurt was first in to bat. Tracy had promised to clock up the score with Belinda to help. For a time Kurt's fours and sixes took up all their attention. Only Holly kept her mind well and truly on Rachel Stone.

'It's OK, I fixed it!' Holly beamed at Belinda and Tracy as the match ended. The sun was already setting along the ridge of the moor. 'I just went across the field to the swimming pool to use the phone. I rang the Manor House. Rachel answered, and she agreed to meet us!'

'She agreed!' Belinda was staggered. 'You've got a nerve, Holly! What if Justin had answered the phone? Or what if Rachel had put the phone down on you and gone and told him it was the same stupid girl pestering her again about the interview?'

Holly shrugged. 'But she didn't.'

'You didn't tell her why you wanted to meet her!' Tracy gasped. 'Like, "Hello, Miss Stone, we think your boyfriend's son is trying to kill me!"'

Holly laughed. 'Of course not. You know me, dead subtle.'

'What did you say then?'

'I said I was terribly sorry, but I'd lost a page of notes I'd made at the original interview. Would she mind if I just went over a few things again?'

'And she agreed?' Tracy asked. 'What a very patient woman Rachel Stone is turning out to be!'

Holly nodded. 'Yes, but we can't meet at the house. She said Mr Mason is due back from London any time, and he likes peace and quiet at weekends. She walks the dogs by the river most evenings, so we fixed a time to meet.'

'When?' Belinda asked.

'Tonight. In twenty minutes, in fact,' Holly said sheepishly.

Excitement gripped them again. They grabbed their bikes, ready to shoot off. Kurt and Simon watched them. Simon shook his head. 'You're asking for it this time,' he said.

Kurt gave him a friendly, consoling nudge. 'Don't worry,' he said, 'you learn to live with it. There's not a thing you can do.'

'That's right!' Holly said with a grin.

The three girls pedalled over the stone bridge, turned right and vanished out of sight.

Rachel greeted them with a friendly wave. She was casually dressed in jeans and a pale blue jacket. Even the dogs bounded up to the girls with joyful recognition while they dismounted from their bikes. Everyone smiled and looked very relaxed. But inside, Holly knew that she and the others trembled on the edge of what they hoped would be their big breakthrough. As they walked, the dogs loped ahead into the woodland lining the river bank, where the town finished and countryside took over.

'So?' Rachel said. 'You lost your notes?'

Holly nodded. 'I couldn't believe I'd been so stupid.'

'Well, I'm relieved to find you're not quite Superwoman!'

'Yet!' Belinda chipped in.

It was all so cheerful, so normal, that it was difficult to see how Holly could steer the conversation towards deadly, dreadful Justin.

Rachel obligingly ran through all the details she thought Holly had lost; how Mr Mason managed to run seven newspapers from his Manor House study, thanks to the miracle of the fax machine. 'You remember, I showed you?'

They walked deeper into the woods. Holly made eye contact with Tracy and Belinda, who recognised the signal.

'Listen,' Tracy said, 'why don't we take the dogs on ahead for a bit of a run? You two can finish off here.'

'Oh, you don't need to do that,' Rachel protested.

'It's no problem. Besides, Belinda needs the

exercise!' Tracy grinned. Belinda raised her eyes, but said nothing. Then they went.

'Watch out for the river just there!' Rachel warned. 'It's narrow down between the rocks. Don't let the dogs jump in. It's deceptive. It's ten metres deep and nothing ever comes up again in one piece!'

Tracy and Belinda nodded. The Great Danes barked for joy. They were quickly out of sight.

'Well?' Rachel turned to Holly. Her smile was open and relaxed.

'Look, I'm really sorry about this,' Holly began.

'Don't worry. I really don't mind running through things again. Anyway, I think I owe you an apology. I hear your departure from the house was less friendly than your arrival.'

'Oh,' Holly said, 'you mean Justin?' Her luck had turned. Here was the topic presented on a plate. 'Did he tell you?'

'Not exactly. I heard the dogs barking and I saw you three beating a hasty retreat. But honestly I don't think they would have harmed you.'

Holly looked doubtful. 'He set them on us, you know.'

Rachel sighed and looked at the ground. 'His idea of a joke, I'm afraid. Anyway, I am very sorry.'

'It's not been my week,' Holly said. Sunshine dappled the grass, and the willow-herb smelt strong and sharp along the shadowy bank. 'I've had, let's see, four narrow escapes!'

'Four!' Rachel stopped in her tracks.

'Well, there was the dogs, which you know about.' Then Holly went on the describe the strange attack at the ice rink. She made it sound like something out of a silent movie; a masterpiece of comic timing. Rachel smiled uneasily. 'Then there was the builders' truck episode,' Holly said. 'I owe my life to my brother and his friend Richard.' Rachel's smile wavered further. She listened in silence. 'Then before that there was the exploding car. That's when it all began.'

Rachel's face had closed right down. She frowned. 'Exploding car?'

'Now the strange thing about that one is that Justin was there too!' Holly let this fact sink in. 'You know, when he crashed his car on the moor? I was there!'

'You were there!' Rachel echoed. The shock made her face look older.

'I was the witness. Dramatic stuff. I saw it go over the edge. That was after he'd forced me off the road, of course. But before the whole thing went up in flames. Anyway, that was just my first narrow escape this week!'

Rachel stared at Holly, shaking her head. 'He was very lucky to escape with his life,' she said.

Holly took the final plunge. 'As a matter of fact, I don't think luck had anything to do with it!' She waited. Rachel half turned away, then came back to listen. 'I think he planned the whole thing, except for my being there, that is.'

'Don't!' Rachel put her hand on Holly's shoulder. 'Please don't go on!' She looked terrified.

'But I'm sure he did. I think he wanted the insurance money. And he wouldn't think twice about harming other people just as long as he got the money!'

Rachel tried once more to shake herself out of the nightmare. 'Don't!' she repeated. 'Even if it's true, please don't!'

'Why not?' Holly asked urgently.

'Because it would harm his father! Mr Mason would never get over it. I have to protect him!'

It was Holly's turn to be shocked by the panic on Rachel's face. 'But surely you can't want Justin to get away with it!' Why was Rachel so frightened? 'Surely it's best to tell Mr Mason the truth!'

Rachel put her hands over her face. 'You don't understand!'

Holly understood one thing: 'It's dangerous to

let Justin go on. He doesn't care who he hurts; me or anyone! Listen, Rachel, you've got to help us! It would be better for everyone if Justin was stopped!'

A little cry escaped through Rachel's trembling fingers. 'No!'

'Why not? You can help! You can come with us to the police and tell them everything you know about Justin, about the insurance money and all the other ways he cheats his father!'

'No!'

'Yes! They won't listen to us. We just need you to back us up!'

'Please!' Tears streamed down Rachel's pale face. 'You don't know what you're asking! You're talking about my . . .' She swallowed back the word. 'It would kill his father! The scandal would kill him!'

'And if you don't help us, he'll kill me!' Holly said, desperate.

Rachel looked up. Something set in her mind, cold and hard. She stopped crying. 'Leave him alone,' she said.

'I can't!'

'Yes, you can. You can stop this silly nonsense right now. And this pretending to be doing research for your schoolwork. It's all nonsense. You've been coming to the Manor House under false pretences. I'm glad Justin set the dogs on you!'

'Rachel!' Holly saw loyalty to her employer get the better of Rachel.

Her grip on Holly's shoulder tightened. Her face was very close. 'Holly, you must stop going round telling these ridiculous stories, do you hear? You must stop snooping and spying, or I'll tell the police!'

'You can't mean that!' Holly stammered. Her voice nearly failed.

'I can. I do!' Rachel stepped back from her. She looked round and clapped her hands smartly for the dogs. They rushed up from the river bank, with Tracy and Belinda close behind. 'Come here!' she called sharply. The dogs came to heel. With one last cold look at Holly, Rachel strode away.

'She said no!' Tracy guessed with one glance at Holly. The girls set off in the other direction, deeper into the woods.

'What happened? Did she warn you off?' Belinda asked.

Holly nodded. 'She said she'd hand us over to the police!'

Tracy gave a low whistle. 'It's OK; no need to tell us any more details,' she said.

They wandered down to the water's edge,

where it ran deep, narrow and fast between smooth grey boulders. The girls stared down into the foaming current. Nearby, a quaint, painted notice gave warning: 'Devil's Leap,' it said. 'The current here is dangerous, and has claimed lives in the past. Please walk carefully.'

11 Not guilty!

'Belinda!' Mrs Hayes's voice came snapping down the phone line. She had on her 'telephone voice,' usually reserved for salespeople and officials from the gas board.

The girls had taken refuge with Meltdown in the stable after another uneasy night. Now they were planning their next move. But much as they ran through the clues in their precious notebook, no obvious action took shape.

'Belinda, there's a very rude boy up here at the house,' Mrs Hayes's voice went on. 'I've no idea who he is, but he's demanding to see you.'

'Ask him his name, will you,' Belinda told her mother. She was in a bad mood. The Mystery Club was well and truly stuck on this case, and without Rachel's help, things were beginning to look pretty hopeless.

'He says he's called Simon Clarke.' Mrs Hayes made the name sound strange and unpleasant, like some slimy creature that had just crawled out of its shell. She was good at expressing disgust. 'He refuses to go!'

'Hang on.' Belinda admitted defeat. 'I'd better go,' she told the others.

'Ahh!' Tracy sighed. 'It's Simon! Lover-boy just can't keep away!'

'Stop that!' Belinda muttered on her way out.

'Such *passion*!' Holly crossed her hands over her heart and joined in making Belinda squirm. It wasn't difficult.

Belinda glared and slammed the door. The others grinned and settled down to wait. But shouting voices drew them out of the stable and up to the house.

'It's all your stupid fault!' Simon was yelling. Belinda backed away down the front lawn. 'You and those two brainless friends of yours playing Sherlock Holmes! And don't say I didn't warn you!'

'Shh!' Mrs Hayes stood at the door in her white silk dressing-gown, on the lookout for neighbours.

'What on earth's wrong?' Holly ran up to Belinda, with Tracy close behind.

'I'll tell you what's wrong!' Simon refused to calm down. His tanned face was red from running and from anger. 'Justin's gone and sacked my mother from her job, that's what's wrong!'

Belinda stood there pale and quiet, flinching at each word. Tracy and Holly were struck dumb.

'Come on, come and see if you don't believe me!' Simon took Belinda's arm. 'She's lost her job, a place to live, everything!'

'Why, what's happened?' Holly found her voice. She tried to step in between Belinda and Simon.

'He says she's not up to the job!' Simon retorted. 'My mum gave him a mouthful when he said that. She's good at her job, even though the pay's rubbish. Anyway, she said stick your job and went straight upstairs to pack. Then Justin tells me he can do anything he likes, and I'd best remember it.'

'Meaning what?' Holly's brain was back in gear now, after the shock of seeing Belinda backing off, pale and silent.

'He says he can hire and fire. His old man can't stop him. Justin's got something on his old man. He's got something on everyone! So he just says to me, laughing, "I've just sacked your old lady, so you'd better find yourselves two old cardboard boxes, 'cos that'll be your home from now on!" I went for him then. But he says it's all my fault for getting mixed up with you three!' Simon paused, running his fingers through his hair. There was a bruise on his forehead where Justin had bashed him.

The girls gasped.

'Nasty!' Tracy muttered.

'He told me, "Tell your friends to lay off, or else!"' He stared at Belinda. Realising he still had hold of her arm, he let it drop.

'How did he know you were seeing us?'

'He knows everything. We were seen together at the cricket match. Justin's friends play for the other side, see. It's a small town. Word gets around.' Simon shrugged.

'But that doesn't mean he has to go and sack your mother!' Belinda protested. 'It's not fair!'

'That's how Justin works. He has to show you he means it.'

'Shh!' Holly said. Mrs Hayes was delicately picking her way across the lawn in her velvet mules.

'Belinda!'

'It's all right, Mum!' She tried in vain to head her off.

'No, it's not all right. What will the neighbours think about all this noise?'

'They can't hear, they're miles away! Anyway, I'm sorry, it's just that Simon's upset about something. His mother's just lost her job.'

'But what's that to do with you?' Mrs Hayes

looked curiously at the group, then sighed. 'It's one of your usual little mysteries, I see. Listen, dear. I'll be late for my squash lesson if I don't hurry and get changed.' She took a last peek at Simon, seemed satisfied, then gave Belinda a peck on the cheek. She trotted back to the house.

'Sorry,' Belinda said, knowing the word was nowhere near enough. 'I never thought that anything like this would happen. It's just not fair!'

'I did try to warn you.' Simon had stopped shouting, but he still wanted someone to blame. 'With Justin you just have to think of the meanest, lowest trick possible and that's what he'll do. You can count on it.'

'What did Rachel say?' Holly asked. 'Is she going to let Justin go ahead and sack your mum?'

'Listen, he went straight to the old man, told him what he'd done. He showed him some receipts or bills that he said my mum had fiddled. The old man believes him. My mum's in tears now. Rachel just stands there in the office!'

'But you're both homeless!' Tracy said.

Holly's determined look had already set in. 'We know he's trying to bump me off,' she declared. 'Now he starts going for someone else!' They had to take some action, and fast. 'Come on!' she said.

'Where to?' Tracy caught her up. Belinda followed with Simon.

'Up to the Manor House, where else?'

'What for?' said Simon.

'To protest!' Holly strode up the hill, past the executive mansions.

'He won't listen,' Simon warned. 'You'll make it worse.'

'It couldn't *be* worse,' Belinda told him miserably. 'You and your mother without a roof over your heads. And it is our fault!' They marched together between the stone lions, up the crazy-paved path.

'This way then!' Simon led them across the terrace, down the side of the house to the stable yard where his mother was packing boxes into an old orange Fiesta. She hardly stopped to look up.

'Here, Simon, give us a hand with this big one!' She heaved and shoved a box on to the back seat. 'Good, that'll do!'

She slammed the door and stood back.

'We're very sorry . . .' Holly began.

'Don't be. I'm not,' Mrs Clarke said, matter of fact. She was gazing up at the house. 'Just give me a second to say cheerio to all those rooms

I've lovingly Hoovered! Good riddance to bad rubbish, that's what we used to say.' She turned and beamed at them.

'But we never meant this to happen,' Holly said, bewildered. Simon was shuffling about behind their backs.

'Listen,' Mrs Clarke told them, 'you three have just done me a very big favour. You've no idea how much I've wanted rid of this job, only I couldn't bring myself to hand in my notice. No courage, see. Then there was Rachel to consider. I'm fond of Rachel. And I suppose I've always had a soft spot for the old man too. But that Justin!' She screwed up her face.

'But Simon came and said you were upset,' Belinda said. 'We came up to see if we could persuade Mr Mason to give you your job back!'

Mrs Clarke roared. 'Well, that's nice of you and I'm sure you mean well.' She grinned at them all. 'I expect I was upset at first. But I don't stay upset for long, do I, Simon? No, I tell you I'm glad to be out of all this!' She reached in her pocket for her car keys. 'My sister will put us up for a week or two while I find myself another job. Plenty of big houses in Willow Dale, and nursing homes and hotels. I'll always find something!'

Relieved, they watched her get into the car. She issued instructions to Simon to make his way down to his aunt's house by lunch-time. 'And thanks again!' she told the girls before she drove off, defiant, through the front entrance.

'Did you ever think you were in the wrong place at the wrong time?' Belinda said, nodding towards the terrace. Mr Mason was advancing towards them.

'Uh-oh,' Holly said.

Then she thought, *What difference does it make? We're here and we've got plenty to say!*

'We'll bring this to a head once and for all,' she said. She felt like a pygmy with a poisoned dart, facing the might of an armoured tank. Mr Mason bore down on them.

He looked at the girls, recognised them, but gave no greeting. He stood face to face with Simon. 'You, you've got half an hour to clear out,' he told him. 'And then that's that, finished. You understand?' It was easy to see how he'd finished up a millionaire newspaperman; he never went back on a decision, never worried about other people's feelings.

Simon coloured up, ready to answer.

'He's not guilty!' Belinda objected. 'And neither is Mrs Clarke! They didn't do anything wrong!'

Mr Mason didn't even look at her. He didn't hear what he didn't want to hear.

'But your son Justin did!' Tracy said.

Then Mr Mason gave a sign. He almost staggered, but then he gathered himself. His voice grew even more formal, more precise. 'I've no time to stand here listening to nonsense. I want you all to leave my premises now! If you don't, I'll call the police!'

'Listen!' Holly saw their chance evaporating. It might never come again. Dark storm-clouds gathered overhead.

Something urgent in her voice deflected the old man's attention. 'I should just turn and walk away from this nonsense!' he said. But for a vital second he hesitated.

'Your son is a dangerous man,' Holly said. 'He's trying to kill me!'

Mr Mason had heard, he couldn't deny it. He stood there, fixed to the spot.

The girls stood their ground. They watched the old man lose height, strength, power. Something faded slowly inside him. Five more seconds and he might have said, 'I know. Everything you say is true.'

But the spell broke. Great dark drops of rain splashed the pale grey stone. Justin himself strode across the terrace and split the group apart. 'Father,' he said in a flat, controlled voice, 'there's a phone call for you in the office.' He snatched the old man from the brink of knowledge. 'It's Paul Dixon in Sheffield. Something about tonight's front page.'

Mr Mason stole one more look at Holly. He shook his head and hurried off to take the call.

Dark drops fell on Justin Mason's dazzling white shirt. He paid no attention to the rain. His stare held them. 'When are you going to realise you're out of your depth?' he asked. 'Or that nobody listens to the truth? No one wants to know the truth.' He smiled. 'Especially if it proves to be inconvenient!'

He was cruel, unhurried. He made them feel young and foolish, like children who'd stayed up too late.

Simon swore, turned on his heel and marched off. The girls still stood steady.

'Apart from which,' Justin continued smoothly, 'you need to learn to value your own safety. Your luck can't hold out forever, you know.'

Holly remembered the hot breath of the monster truck, the icy spray from the silver blades. But now this was a cooler Justin, more determined than ever, more dangerous.

'Safety depends altogether on the people you know,' he explained. 'Me, I know all the top men. I'm very safe. I also know all the crooks and car thieves, all the thugs who skulk around the bottom of the pile. Who do you know?'

Why was he telling them this, giving them this lesson in intimidation, Holly wondered. Why was he explaining and showing off?

'And I know all about you three!' He looked at them one by one.

It was true, they felt it deep down; he did.

'I know about your families; where they get their money, who gives them their jobs.' He shook his head, looking at Holly. 'Your father makes very beautiful furniture. I've seen it. In fact, I bought a table. It's in my room. Very beautiful.'

Holly remembered the hours of care, the chipping and carving, the shaving, the sanding, the smell of resin as her father worked. She felt angry that it was wasted on people like Justin.

'He has valuable hands, your father.'

Holly lurched suddenly from anger into fear. The suggestion was there in Justin's evil, flat voice, the visions of damage; broken bones, slashed fingers. She backed off. He meant it. This man knew no limits, and his 'friends' would do anything he paid them to do. It was too much to fight.

Holly saw Tracy and Belinda catch up with his meaning. She realised that Tracy's mother had small children in the nursery, and that Belinda's father often flew in a private plane. All were vulnerable.

He saw how much he'd scared them now. At last they understood.

Rain poured down. It bounced off the stone. It drenched their hair and trickled down their scalps. Swiftly Justin turned and walked back into the house.

12 A plea for help

This time the Mystery Club decided to retreat to the safety of Holly's room. Mr Adams was in his workshop, chiselling away at a pale oak coffee table. 'Get dry, you three,' he yelled. 'You look like drowned rats!'

Jamie thought it was hilarious. He scuttled round the kitchen making rat noises.

'Get lost, Jamie!' Holly warned. Gratitude for saving her life had already worn pretty thin.

Safe in Holly's room, the girls dried off and stopped shivering. They looked at one another, rain-washed and bedraggled. 'You scared?' Holly asked the others.

They nodded.

'Me too.' There didn't seem much else to say, but the silence gave Justin Mason total power over their minds.

'Put some music on,' Tracy suggested. 'Something loud and mindless.'

For ten minutes they tried to drown their fears in guitars and drums.

'Dad says turn that noise down!' Jamie hammered at the door. 'He can't hear himself think.'

'Exactly!' Holly glared at her brother. But she turned the volume down anyway. In another five minutes Mr Adams appeared at the door with a tray of hot chocolate and biscuits. 'To help you warm up,' he said kindly.

'Thanks, Dad.' She took the tray.

'Anything wrong? You look as if you all need cheering up.'

'No. we're fine, thanks,' Holly said, trying to sound cheerful. If he went on being nice she might lose her nerve and tell him everything. Then their investigation would collapse.

'OK. I'm down in the workroom if you need me.' Mr Adams smiled and closed the door on them.

'I'm still shaking,' Belinda complained.

'But we've got to act normal,' Tracy said. 'We must pull ourselves together!'

When the phone went, it shredded their nerves again. 'Holly, it's for you!' Jamie yelled up the stairs.

'Who is it?' Holly whispered at him as she went down to answer.

129

'Some woman,' Jamie shrugged. He shot back into the living-room to watch TV.

'Hello?' She wondered who it could be.

'Hello, Holly. This is Rachel Stone.'

Holly sat down on the bottom step, suddenly weak-kneed. She beckoned Tracy and Belinda downstairs. 'Is something the matter?' The last she recalled was Rachel standing by Devil's Leap threatening to call the police. And things certainly hadn't improved since then.

Rachel held on to a long silence. When she spoke again her voice sounded strange and uneven. 'I'm not sure. Yes, everything's terrible, but I can't tell you on the phone. I've been thinking about what you told me down by the river. And some awful things are happening here now too. My . . . Mr Mason is ill. He's in bed, very sick. I don't know what to do. I just think something dreadful is going to happen!' Now her voice broke down completely.

'Listen, Rachel, what do you want us to do?' Holly hated to hear the panic and fear. She wanted Rachel to be her efficient, light and lovely self. Tracy and Belinda had crowded round to listen. 'Do you want us to go to the police and tell them everything?' Holly asked.

'No!' It was like mercury shooting up a thermometer, the panic in her voice. 'You mustn't do

130

that. But could you come here? I can't come out to meet you. I can't leave him alone here.'

'What about Justin?' Holly asked. A third meeting with him at the Manor House was to be avoided at all costs.

'He's not here. He's gone out for the evening. Look, I'm absolutely sure he won't be back, otherwise I wouldn't ask. Please come!'

Holly looked at Belinda and Tracy for an answer. 'Just a minute,' she said down the phone. Then, 'Well?'

'It could be a trap,' Tracy said. 'Why has she suddenly changed her mind about us?'

'It doesn't sound like she's faking it,' Belinda said. 'She sounds really scared.'

'We can't refuse,' Holly said. 'Not now.' If things were getting worse for Rachel Stone, it was at least partly due to the Mystery Club's investigations. If Justin Mason was throwing his weight around up at the Manor House, it was their fault this time.

Holly took her hand off the mouthpiece. 'OK, we'll come up to the house,' she said, 'as long as Justin's not there. If he comes back you'll have to warn us, OK? We can't risk upsetting him any more than we already have.'

'Of course, of course, I understand!' Rachel

sounded terribly relieved. 'How long will you be?'

'About half an hour.'

'Good. Please hurry. Please come as quickly as you can!'

The phone went dead. Holly, Belinda and Tracy grabbed their wet anoraks from the kitchen hooks and headed out into the rain.

The bike ride up to the Manor House was a wet and miserable journey along the swollen riverside, through the town and up through Belinda's executive estate towards the old house in its wooded grounds.

The moorside loomed grey above them, the colour of lead. The girls cycled with grim determination until the bleak walls came into sight. The stone lions seemed half dissolved in mist and rain; the iron gates dripped.

'Hide the bikes,' Holly said, 'just in case.'

They took them into the stable yard and propped them out of sight against a wall under a lean-to shed. Their feet scrunched on the wet gravel. Warily they looked for any sign of Justin's sleek black car.

'If it wasn't for that car!' Belinda muttered.

'I know. It's the cause of all the trouble,' Holly agreed. 'Anyway, it's not here, so we're safe.' They went round and rang the front doorbell.

Rachel Stone answered the door, but they scarcely recognised her. She was dishevelled, red-eyed and frightened, her blonde hair stuck to her cheeks. She gasped out her thanks as she let them in. 'Thank goodness!' she cried. 'I was so worried!'

They went in. 'Justin's still out?' Tracy checked.

'Yes, and I wish he'd never come back!'

The great door closed loudly on the dim hall. 'This way.' Rachel led them into the office.

'What's happened?' Tracy was the most impatient. She still suspected a trap, with Justin hidden in every alcove.

Rachel shook her head. 'Keep your voices down, please. Mr Mason's sleeping, but the least sound could wake him.'

'What's wrong with him?' Holly asked. 'Just tell us what's happened. Why did you ask us to come up here?'

'I don't know exactly what's wrong,' Rachel began. 'He won't talk to me. He's just taken to his bed. He won't eat. He's not had a thing to eat since he came back on Sunday evening.'

'Have you called the doctor?'

'He won't let me. He absolutely refuses.' Rachel turned to Holly. 'What did you say to him? I think it might be something you said.'

'Look!' Tracy stepped in, ready to defend Holly, but Holly held her back.

'It's OK.' She looked Rachel straight in the face. 'I told him his son was trying to kill me. I told him the truth.'

Rachel sat limply in Mr Mason's big leather chair and leaned on his desk. 'What did he say?'

With a little laugh Holly told her. 'He threatened me with the police! It's funny, everyone here goes around warning me they'll call the police!'

'I'm sorry.' Rachel looked up. 'What did he do then?'

'Justin came out in the nick of time and took him off to answer the phone.'

'And since then he's refused to talk to anyone. Not a word!' Rachel stood up and looked out across the wet lawn. 'But that's not all.' She turned to face them. 'I know this sounds ridiculous, but I think it's more than that. I haven't any proof, and it sounds half crazy. I mean, Justin is his son!' She broke down and leaned on the desk.

'What sounds half crazy?' Holly said gently. She was prepared to believe what Rachel told her, however wild.

'I think Justin's trying to kill his father! He's poisoning him. He's making him ill somehow, I know he is!'

Tracy gasped and turned to Belinda.

'Shh!' Belinda warned.

Holly considered it carefully. 'When did you first begin to think this?' She tried not to sound shocked, though the idea took her breath away.

'A week ago, maybe ten days. I don't know. Anyway, after he crashed his car and things got so bad here. All those rows about money. Mr Mason tried to get tough with Justin. It was from then onwards. He started not eating. I think he was sick a lot, but he didn't tell anyone. You'd have to know him very well to see that something was wrong!'

Rachel hung her head and cried, then pulled herself back together. 'Anyway, I knew he was ill. Then he went to London for those few days, and Justin was sorting out this stupid insurance business and got his new car, so I thought things might be better when Mr Mason got back. But then you three seemed to be upsetting Justin all the time, and poor Mrs Clarke got the sack, and Mr Mason didn't seem any better. In fact, he got worse! He's so poorly, I don't know what to do!'

'How could Justin be poisoning him?' Belinda asked. 'When would he get the opportunity?'

Rachel battled against tears to go on with the story. 'He takes some pills for a heart condition. He's been told it's not serious, but the doctor keeps an eye on him. I've thought about it. I spent all of last night thinking about it. And suddenly I remembered how Justin will always remind his father to take his pills.'

'Is that unusual?'

For a second Rachel looked almost calm. 'Justin isn't exactly famous for his concern and consideration.'

'No,' Belinda agreed.

'So, I wondered about it for a long time.' The distraught tone had returned. 'I remembered he went to collect the last prescription from the chemist. I suppose it's possible that Justin has meddled with the dosage or something!' Then as if the possibility was too dreadful, she shook her head and laughed. 'Probably not. I'm probably just being sensational!'

The girls listened. The mist was rolling down from the moortop, shrouding the house and muffling the sound of the rain falling. Inside, the nightmare took a new shape. 'Is this why you've asked us to come?' Holly said.

Rachel nodded. She straightened her hair, and pulled her long jumper neatly down over her trousers. 'I wanted to tell someone. But I see now it's all ridiculous. I've just worked myself up into a state, that's all!' She began to apologise for her fears and suspicions. 'Only I was so worried about him!'

'It may not be all that ridiculous,' Holly said. 'From what we know about Justin,' she added.

Rachel's face quivered. Her fine brows knotted and she drew a deep breath.

'I think you were right to tell us,' Belinda confirmed.

They sank into deep thought. The stakes had risen. More lives were in danger. The danger was doubling and redoubling as each day passed.

'Will you take me up to see Mr Mason?' Holly said at last. 'We have to convince him that his life's in danger. We have to make him listen.'

It was as if she'd asked to stick a knife into the sick man. Rachel recoiled. I can't. I have to protect him. I've always protected him from Justin!'

'But don't you see that protecting him from the truth isn't good for him? It might even be killing him!'

Rachel struggled with her conscience. 'All right, you can try,' she said slowly. 'Just Holly.' She signalled the others to wait, and led her through the gloomy hall, up to Mr Mason's bedroom.

It was a room without a woman's touch. There was an old four-poster bed without drapes to soften its edges. There were books on shelves, but no ornaments or flowers. The walls were plain and dark, decorated with old maps and prints.

The lamps were on low. Rachel went over to draw the curtains against the fading light, and the room grew drearier, the shadows deeper. Holly had to stare hard at the huge bed before she could make out details of Mr Mason's figure, lying face up, shrouded in white.

'He's asleep,' Rachel whispered. 'We ought not to disturb him.' She started to retreat.

But the old man's eyes opened, like holes burnt into parchment. His face didn't move as his eyes followed Rachel around the room. 'Who's there?'

'It's only me.' Rachel smiled as best she could. 'How are you feeling?' She put her hand against the lined, yellowish face. 'Do you feel better after your sleep?'

Mr Mason made an effort to nod. 'Don't fuss, Rachel. There's no need. You know I don't want a fuss.' He tried to soften his voice and smile.

'You know I've never had a day's illness in my life before.' He sighed. 'I'd like some water, please.'

While Rachel went to refill the glass with cool, fresh water, Holly approached the bed. She saw how ill Mr Mason was, and she nearly weakened. She felt it would be cruel to disturb him. But the dark, feverish eyes recognised her and now it was too late.

'Rachel!' His voice had lost volume, but it was still authoritative.

'Here. I'm here.' She hurried back, trying to smile, trying to soothe.

'Get her out of here!' He struggled to raise his head, but he was too weak. 'What is she doing here? Get her out!'

'No.' Holly stood firm. 'Mr Mason, you must listen to me now. You didn't believe me before, but you must believe me now!'

He closed his eyes and turned his head away.

'Yes, you must. It's very important. It's about Justin again. Rachel phoned me. She's worried he might be trying to harm you now!'

The old man turned to look at Holly, pleading with her. 'I've not been fair to Justin,' he said, trying to find an excuse for his son. 'I haven't treated him well. I spent too much time away, even when he was little. Even when his mother died. It's my fault!'

'No!' Holly insisted. 'He's a grown man; he's not a child. He's trying to kill you and he's harming others! You mustn't let him.'

But the weight of twenty years' guilt pressed down on the old man. 'I shouldn't have stopped his allowance!'

'He's using you, Mr Mason!' Holly grew desperate.

'He's my son!'

'He's trying to poison you!' Holly declared at last.

She saw a powerful man robbed of his power, a successful man whose success had crumbled. What would he do now that he'd been told the truth?

Edward Mason's eyes flashed, his throat clamped tight and his breath rasped. From his mouth poured a stream of croaked anger. Rachel's hands flew to her face and she backed out of the room.

'Mr Mason, listen to me!' Holly stepped forward.

He sat bolt upright in his anger. 'Did she let you in? Did she?' His eyes rolled wildly, looking for Rachel.

'No, it was my idea!' Holly tried to stop

140

him getting out of bed. 'Please calm down, Mr Mason!'

But still the angry words poured out. Holly fled from the room.

13   *Living a lie*

Holly followed Rachel, who ran quickly up to
the attics, to Mrs Clarke's old room. It was
almost stripped of furniture, dark and bare in
the gloomy, gathering night.

'Can I come in?'

Rachel didn't answer. She knelt on the floor
and held on to a cushion from the remaining
chair, clutching it as a child might hug a doll for
comfort.

'I'm sorry.' Holly went over and knelt beside
her. 'What do you want to do now?'

Rachel shook her head. She rocked slowly
backwards and forwards.

'You have to call the doctor,' Holly advised
gently. When she still got no reply, she tried a
firmer line. 'He's very ill. If you care anything at
all about Mr Mason, you must call the doctor!'

Rachel looked up with desperate eyes. 'Care
about him?'

'Yes. Mrs Clarke said something about . . .

Well, it's obvious you do care. Anyone can see that you do.' Even now, even when the man's life was at stake, it was awkward to bring the matter out into the open.

'Of course I care!' Rachel had sprung up and thrust the cushion away. 'How could I not care?'

'Maybe you don't want to talk about it. It's not my business. But saving him from Justin is!'

Face to face, Holly was nearly crushed by the new fierceness in Rachel's stare.

'What do you mean, talk about it? Talk about what? What are you suggesting?'

'That you and Mr Mason are having an affair,' Holly said in a quiet, scared voice.

Rachel's sharp laugh of realisation was squeezed dry of every drop of humour. 'Oh, I see . . . You think I – You think he – Oh, how ridiculous!'

'I'm sorry,' Holly murmured. It was a stupid mistake; she saw that now. 'It's just that Mrs Clarke said you were fond of each other.'

'Listen, listen!' Rachel said, taking Holly by the shoulder. 'I have to put a stop to this. Is that what they're saying? Oh, the poor man!' She kept shaking her head in disbelief. 'It's not true!'

'No?'

'Of course not! I'm not his mistress. How could I be? I'm his daughter!'

Silence swam around the room. Darkness drowned them. Way below a clock chimed.

'I'm his illegitimate daughter!' Rachel repeated.

Suddenly the story rearranged itself. It was like dropping a stitch of knitting and having everything unravel. Holly had to start again. 'You're Justin's sister?'

'Half-sister.'

'Younger?'

'Four years younger. My mother had an affair with my father, with Mr Mason, when he was still married to Justin's mother. She came to work for him when he was just setting up in Sheffield, just making a name for himself. They would work late in the office, the usual thing, getting the early editions ready. My mother had never met anyone like him. She was in love with him. She would have gone to the ends of the earth for him!'

'And Mr Mason?' Holly, enthralled by the story, whispered in the dark.

'I think he loved her.'

'But?'

'He had a wife. He said he needed time to decide. He had a son. She waited six months, maybe a year. Then, when she was pregnant with me, she left. She left the job without telling him, just left. She never told him.

Eventually she got a job in London. We moved from flat to flat, and somehow she made ends meet.'

'Didn't she ever ask him for any money?'

Rachel shook her head. Her grip on Holly had loosened. 'She was too proud. She began to do well writing features for glossy magazines. I had a good childhood, a wonderful one. My mother treated me like an equal. I met interesting people; journalists, celebrities. Then she got ill. Cancer. I was in my last year at school. Finally she wrote to my father and told him he had a daughter, me.' Rachel's voice had reached vanishing point.

'What did he do?'

'He came to see us. My mother was already ill. He asked her why she never contacted him, even after she must have known his wife had died. My mother just said it was something he would never understand. He said he'd make it up to her. But it was too late.' Rachel wept.

'He still wanted desperately to make it up. But my mother died. I said I would come up here with him to work, but not as his daughter. That's the way my mother would've wanted it. I'd come, as long as the secret was safe. He promised. He would have done anything to make up for the past.'

'And what about you?' They stood together by the window, looking down.

'He's my father. I love him.'

'And what about Justin?'

'He hates me. He says he'll reveal our secret, he'll show the world what a lie his respectable father lives. Every time my father tries to cut back on what Justin spends, or tries to keep him in line, he threatens him. Then my father tries to protect me; as if I cared about scandal, about what other people think!'

'But he does?'

'Yes. His whole world depends on it. He couldn't bear to be found out. That's his weakness, really. His strength and his weakness; Edward Mason, the rock of respectability.'

'Yes.' Holly recalled the stiff back, the iron willpower, the story of the poor boy made good. 'So Justin holds this power over him?'

'And a grudge against me. He thinks I'm going to inherit some of the money, the house. I don't know.' She shook her head. 'Anyway, he hates me.'

'Has Mr Mason altered his will for you?'

'I won't let him.'

'Have you told Justin that?'

'Yes. At first he didn't believe us, but Father showed him a copy of the will. There it is in black and white: Justin Mason, sole beneficiary. So then Justin had to believe it. Until a couple of weeks ago, when the car business happened. Father couldn't stand any more of Justin cheating and stealing. There was a terrible, terrible row. He stopped Justin's allowance. He said this was his last chance. Next time he'd change his will. He'd leave everything to me!'

'One last chance?'

Rachel nodded. 'Justin knows he means it. My father's reached the end of his tether. That's why Justin's trying to kill him now, before he can alter his will!'

Holly agreed. She thought of the poor, sick man in his four-poster bed.

'Justin has this thing about money. He won't let go of a single penny. It's all his, and he wants more!' Rachel shook her head in despair.

'He has habits,' Holly reminded her. She saw it all now. It all made sense.

'An expensive girlfriend called Jackie Severne,' Rachel told her. 'A glamourous, beautiful redhead. Married, though. She expects a lot from Justin, and somehow she gets it! She's the only one who can persuade him to do things. It's strange; he'll do anything to keep her, buy her whatever she wants; clothes, jewellery, holidays. It's a kind of obsession with him.'

147

'But you say she's married?'

'That just makes him more determined to impress her. It's like a competition. She's a trophy he wants to win from her husband.'

'And have his name engraved on her?' Holly suggested.

Rachel smiled weakly. 'Why have I told you all this?'

'You had to tell someone. Come on, let's go down.' She offered to take Rachel's hand.

'What shall we do now?'

'Make that phone call. Your father needs a doctor, and he needs one now.'

They went down, gathering courage as they turned on the lights and banished the shadows. Rachel called the doctor's emergency number, while Holly joined Belinda and Tracy in Mr Mason's office. She nodded at them excitedly. 'Justin's pushed his luck once too often,' she told them. 'Now we're going to be able to put a stop to him once and for all!'

When the doorbell rang, they rushed to it, expecting the doctor Rachel had phoned.

Rachel opened the door. Jackie Severne stood there in a halo of mist and rain.

The girls stepped back in disbelief.

'Is Justin here?' The woman ignored them. She

stepped inside and shook her mane of red hair. 'Well?'

Jackie's fingernails were red, so was her lipstick. Her stiletto shoes were black and red. The rest was dramatic black against her pale skin; black beaded top, black velvet skirt.

'He's gone out. Did you arrange to meet him here?' Rachel tried to sound calm.

'Obviously I did, for goodness' sake!' Jackie glanced around the room, as if she suspected Rachel of lying. 'We said we'd meet here. What time is it?'

'Eight o'clock. Justin went off over an hour ago. He was meeting Steve Ward at the golf club, I think.'

Jackie's tantrum worsened. She tossed her head, stared into the office at Holly and the others as if it was their fault, and flounced out into the hall again. 'I'm sure he didn't say golf club to me! Just ring him, will you? Tell him I'm here.'

She waited for Rachel to obey her order, then changed her mind. 'No, wait a minute, I can hear a car!'

Headlights swept down the driveway, then died outside the front door.

'That's Justin now!' Jackie Severne smiled like a beauty queen. 'I knew he'd come back for me!'

The girls stood rooted to the spot. The nightmare had come true. They heard the car door slam with a sense of doom.

Holly roused herself first. She looked wildly round and headed for the room they knew: the office. 'This way!' She pulled Tracy and Belinda after her.

Justin swept in past Rachel, with Steve Ward close on his heels. The truck driver had acquired a name, but he still looked uncomfortable in a suit. Rachel faded into the shadows as Justin took Jackie in his arms.

In Mr Mason's study, the Mystery Club closed their eyes and prayed. If ever they needed a miracle, they needed it now!

Please let him sweep right out the house with Jackie Severne on his arm! Please let him not come in here!

14 Kidnap!

'The patio door!' Tracy pointed to the French windows. They scrambled past the computers and the telephones, fumbled with the handle, managed the Yale lock. They escaped into the wet, dark night. Quietly Tracy clicked the door shut behind them.

'Let's get out of here!' Belinda said. Her eyes began to adjust to the darkness. The Mystery Club could cut diagonally across the stone terrace, through the neat rose beds, and take a final risk by going out through the front gate. By then it would be too late for anyone to stop them.

'No,' Holly whispered. 'We can't just leave Rachel and Mr Mason!'

Rain dripped noisily from the eaves on to the stone flags. There was no moon, but the mist had cleared from the ground.

'Why not?' Tracy said, eager to put some distance between them and Justin. 'This is one of those times when you just have to run!'

'Rachel can't look after her father alone!'

Holly began to make her way round the side of the house, keeping out of the pools of light shed by the windows.

'Her *what*?' Belinda kept close by her side.

'Her father,' Holly repeated. 'Mr Mason is Rachel's father. I'll explain later.'

She thought they'd get the best view from Simon's old workroom in the stable block and she led the others there. 'He's very ill. I finally persuaded Rachel to call the doctor.' She explained that the doctor was due any time. 'If Justin's still here, he won't let him in the house. We've got to stick around, just in case.'

She bundled Belinda and Tracy into the room full of saddles and boots, where at least it was dry. They crouched behind the door. 'We can't let Justin win,' Holly whispered. 'Not now!'

Minutes ticked by. The rain continued to pour down. The house stood prison-like with its black walls and small windows. The girls watched and waited.

Then the French windows of the study burst open. A small pane of glass shattered and fell on to the stone. An enraged Justin had flung the doors wide open. They swung wildly on their hinges. He stood silhouetted against the lamplight, legs wide apart. 'Where are they?' he

152

yelled. 'You say they were in here. Well, where are they now?' He strode along the terrace.

Jackie tottered out into the rain. 'They've gone,' she said, trying to calm him. 'They're only a bunch of kids. What harm can they do?'

'Plenty.' He went back inside to turn on an outdoor light. The terrace shone yellow and wet. Light spilled over the rose beds. The stables were still in darkness.

'Oh, for goodness' sake!' Jackie complained. 'Just look at the rain. It'll ruin my hair!'

'Poor you!' Justin said, but he didn't sound sympathetic.

She ignored him. 'I'd never have mentioned any of this if I'd known. Don't you think you're overreacting a tiny little bit?'

'Shut it, will you!'

Justin strode savagely down the garden path. He yelled for Rachel. 'Get yourself out here! Get looking! It's all your stupid fault letting them in the house in the first place!' He grabbed her by the shoulder and pushed her ahead of him.

'You'll wake him, you'll wake him!' she pleaded. 'I'll help you look, only please, please don't shout. You'll upset him!' She looked back upstairs towards Mr Mason's dimly-lit room. Then she and Justin spread out in different directions. Steve Ward stood on the terrace, holding the Great Danes on their leashes. He was wider than Justin, not so tall, standing with legs braced, ignoring the rain.

'Told you we should've run away!' Tracy whispered.

'Shh!' Holly saw Justin vault back on to the terrace to confer with Steve Ward.

'Rachel can take the front of the house,' he said. 'And I'll take the shrubbery down by the wall. You take a look in the stable yard.' He looked like thunder. Meanwhile, Jackie Severne stood in the study, tossing her head, tapping her fingernails.

'Here, give me the dogs,' Justin ordered. Then he vanished into the dark shadows by the wall. Holly could hear him beating savagely at the bushes as he went. Steve Ward headed in their direction, alone.

'Get down!' Holly whispered.

'Hope he doesn't spot the bikes!' Tracy shot a look across the yard to the lean-to.

'Over here!' Belinda whispered. They crawled after her through the door which joined the workroom to the stable. 'In here, in here!' she said. Holly and Tracy crawled deep into the straw while Belinda whispered and sweet-talked an enormous grey stallion, the occupant of the stable. Its hooves were as big as saucers.

Tracy and Holly curled up in the straw, while the horse gently stirred, then settled. Just in time; Steve Ward's tread echoed through the yard. He opened the workroom door and fumbled for the light, just as Belinda slid down into the far corner of the stable, whisking straw over herself for camouflage.

The man felt for the light switch. He tramped across the room and tried again. Then he spotted an old anglepoise lamp fixed to a shelf. He groped for it and flicked the switch. The workroom was flooded with light. From next door they could see him wrench the light from its mooring and carry it high around the room, poking into corners.

The big grey lifted its hooves and tossed its head. It shoved restlessly against the side of its stall. The girls curled up smaller, pressed against the walls.

Ward held the light high, considered the stallion, then began to edge towards it. Holly, Belinda and Tracy scarcely breathed under the straw. The man examined the stable shadows. He swung the light forward.

Then there was a second wrench and everything went black. Ward swore again, something fell and the horse clattered its hooves. He had pulled the light from its socket and left himself in darkness. In disgust, he flung the lamp down, backed off from the angry, invisible beast in the stable and sought the fresh air. The horse snorted and clattered, the man's footfalls retreated. The girls breathed again.

'Good boy,' Belinda said softly, calming the horse again. 'Good, good boy!' She stood up and spoke kind words close to its blowing nostrils. It settled, whisked its tail and listened.

Holly and Tracy stood up at last, brushing off the straw. 'Good boy!' they said, nervously patting its enormous neck. When all was quiet, they emerged into the yard. Keeping to the shadows, they crept back towards the terrace.

'No luck?' Justin was checking with Steve Ward. 'You mean we've lost them?'

'They'd get out double quick if they know what's good for them,' Ward shrugged and brushed the wet from his shoulders. 'So I vote we go on from here.'

Justin stared fiercely into the darkness. 'You go on ahead,' he ordered. 'Take Jackie with you.'

'Oh, Justin!' the light voice protested. 'How much longer are you going to be hanging on here?'

He leaned inside the study to calm her down. 'Steve will go on ahead with you,' he said. 'I booked a table at Scott's for nine. A surprise.

I won't be long. I just have a couple of things to sort out with Rachel.' Justin waved the others back.

It was all quiet until the front door opened. Jackie and Steve came out. She still didn't look happy. 'Don't be long,' she said, pouting. 'You know how much I hate hanging around waiting!'

She teetered forwards into the driver's seat of her own car. Steve took the passenger seat.

Justin waved them off. Jackie's car disappeared, too fast, down the driveway. The headlights hit the stone lions full beam, swung out of the gate and vanished. Justin closed the front door, came round the outside of the house, took one last look in the garden, gave up and went in through the French windows. He closed them tight.

Holly looked at the others. For a couple of minutes everything went quiet.

'What now?' Belinda asked. They were all soaked.

'Where's that doctor?' Tracy complained.

Holly shook her head. 'No, we want to get rid of Justin before the doctor arrives.' She turned back to the house. 'Oh, no, what's going on?'

Inside Mr Mason's office a fresh scene had

developed, this time with the volume turned right down. The three girls found themselves drawn across the terrace, closer and closer, watching the dumb show.

The door from the hall into the study had opened. Mr Mason himself stood there, ghostly pale. He had his hand on the doorknob, leaning on it for support.

Rachel rushed to steady him. He looked dazed. Justin pulled her to one side. He was ordering the old man back upstairs. Mr Mason shook his head. Rachel tried again to get to her father. Justin was shouting. The old man raised a powerless fist.

Rachel grabbed Justin, who flung her away like a rag doll. She fell helplessly against a desk. From the floor she was saying *no*, *no*, struggling to her feet.

Justin advanced on his father. Rachel shouted something that stopped him in his tracks. He swung round, caught hold of her, pushed her backwards towards the glass panes of the French doors. With a great heave he flung her against them. They burst open a second time. She fell out into the rain. Justin's fury was loosed upon the night.

'Say that again, you stupid fool!' He leapt out and wrenched her to her feet. 'You told them everything! You told those kids the truth! Go on, say it again!' He had one hand cupped under Rachel's chin, forcing her head back.

'I told Holly about my father!' she cried. The old man staggered to the smashed doors and stood propped there, broken and exhausted.

The force of Justin's shove lifted her off her feet again, but she picked herself up. She'd said it out loud. The secret was spoken. 'I told her the truth,' she repeated calmly. 'I'm not scared any more. Do your worst!'

Holly, Belinda and Tracy watched the floodlit scene, and now they could hear it too. They heard old Mr Mason cry out. 'Rachel, you mustn't!' he said. 'Don't tell anyone. You don't know what people will do to us!' He hardly had the strength to lift himself over the threshold. 'Rachel!' he cried. 'Tell them it's not true. Say you lied!'

'Father, it's not like that any more!' she cried out, desperate.

But Justin was backing off from her, sneering, saying, 'Who's going to believe you, anyway? You and those three kids? They'll say you're just a gold-digger. A dirty little liar. That's what you are!'

'No!' Rachel's face grew desperate again. 'It's the truth! They'll have to believe us!' She appealed to the old man. 'Don't let him do this to us!'

Justin straightened his jacket. 'You heard him. He'll deny it.' He looked with contempt at the old man. 'If he lives long enough, that is.'

And that was when Holly leapt forward. Her heart surged with anger against this cruelty. She raced towards the terrace.

Inside the house the dogs barked. Justin swung round to face her. Tracy and Belinda followed, trying to pull her back.

'Liar!' Holly shouted at the top of her voice. She leapt up and struck Justin in the chest. Rachel cried out. Mr Mason staggered against the wall.

'Liar!' Holly yelled again. Justin hauled her off her feet and flung her backwards towards Belinda and Tracy.

Holly's angry protest had snapped Justin back into another frenzy of anger. He snarled as he hauled Holly back where she'd come from and whipped round to fend off Rachel as she too came running at him. The back of his hand smashed into her face. She jerked heavily forward to clutch her cheek. He caught her neck in the crook of his elbow and began dragging her sideways. 'Don't move!' he commanded, looking straight at Holly. 'If you move, she's dead!'

Holly froze. There was a moan from the old man, but no other noise. They stood like statues as Justin dragged Rachel, struggling and half choking, across to the drive. The shadows swallowed the two figures.

'Don't move!' his voice yelled from the darkness. They heard car doors open and close and the engine fire into life. Justin's headlights lit the terrace and caught the girls and Mr Mason frozen in their beams. The lights swung across the ivy-covered walls of the house as Justin reversed his car. Then he pitched forward down the drive.

The car that Justin had been willing to cheat, lie and even kill for shot away. Inside it was a madman and an innocent woman.

15 Wild water

Screaming tyres brought figures running across the long lawns. They leapt out of Justin's way as he roared out between the gates.

'What's going on here?' Simon and Kurt had been worried about the girls and come looking for them up at the Manor House. The sounds of breaking glass and screeching tyres only brought them running more quickly through the wet, dark night.

'Belinda, what's going on?' Simon demanded, standing in her way.

But the girls had no time to explain. They had to keep track of Justin and follow on their bikes. Already his headlights were snaking across the dark moorside.

'Simon, look after Mr Mason. The doctor's on his way!' Belinda yelled. The others were already astride of their bikes. She followed.

Simon saw the old man slumped on the terrace; a dark heap amongst the splintered glass glinting in the lamplight. 'Come on!' he yelled.

Simon and Kurt headed over the garden as the Mystery Club set their bikes downhill, desperate to keep Justin's car in sight.

They leaned forward, the rain lashing their faces. They saw the headlights dipping and lurching, but always stretching the gap between them, as the girls pedalled at breakneck speed.

Then they heard another screeching of brakes ahead, another bend and the scraping of metal. There was another set of headlights, but these were heading up the hill. The two cars swerved, ricocheted against the walls and scraped past each other. Justin's car spun across the road and righted itself with difficulty. It gave Holly and the others a few precious seconds' advantage. The other car had ground to a halt when they reached the spot. A man stood by his car in the rain, inspecting the damage.

'Doctor Goodwin?' Belinda braked, still last of the group. She recognised him from the Willow Dale health centre. 'You're needed up at the Manor House. It's Mr Mason; he's very ill!' Then she was past, flying after Holly and Tracy. The doctor leapt back into his car. 'And call the police!' Belinda yelled.

There was silence as the girls pedalled in top

gear, bent forward over their handlebars like speed riders. They followed the shimmering headlights and the whine of Justin's car engine.

They shot down the hill between black walls glistening with rain, and across the moor. They cut behind the town on a minor road, heading for the valley bottom. Justin raced along this lonely road with his unwilling passenger. For a mile, two miles, three, they pedalled until their lungs nearly burst, desperate to keep him in sight.

Then suddenly the headlights cut out and the engine died.

Apart from the whir of their own tyres, the night went ghostly quiet.

'Where is he?' Tracy gasped. She was ahead of the others. Overhead trees cut out what little light they'd had. It was like cycling into tar. 'Where are we?'

'Stride Woods, I think,' Belinda said. The beech trees arched over them. 'Down by the river. Listen.' They heard the rush of water.

'Quiet!' Holly had heard car doors slam over to their right, muffled and some distance away. 'This way!'

They left the road for a rough track down to a lonely car park. There, slewed against the fence in a huge arc of skidmarks, was Justin's abandoned car.

164

'Come on!' Holly yelled. She flung down her bike, checked the car and raced on through a gate.

'Where to?' Tracy leapt the fence. 'You sure this is right?' Belinda came steadily behind.

Holly nodded. She ran ahead through ankle deep mud down a footpath bordered by giant trees. There were recent footprints just visible; a man's and a woman's.

Grim-faced, they raced on. In a gap in the trees, through a rare break in the clouds, they passed a notice, like a gallows silhouetted in the moonlight.

They read the sign: 'Devil's Leap. The current here is dangerous, and has claimed lives in the past . . .'

Of course; the roaring water, the dripping woods. Where else could it be? Holly pulled the others up, motioned them to go carefully. They were very near the river now, their ears drowned in the fury of the water.

'Wait!' Holly stopped. There were no trees for cover, just an open expanse of moss-covered rocks, treacherously slippery after all the rain. And there, at the water's edge, poised over the cauldron, were Justin and Rachel.

Holly felt her heart thundering. She was certain Justin must have heard or seen them, but he didn't look round. The girls crept forward.

The wild water frothed at Justin's feet. He held Rachel, her head forced back in the crook of his arm as before, only now she didn't struggle.

'You see this?' he yelled. He swung her nearer to the edge. 'You know where we are?'

She tried to nod.

'A favourite suicide spot! You jump in here and nobody ever comes up again – except as a corpse, when the rains go down!'

He was mad. Nothing could stop him. They saw Rachel weaken, then brace herself.

Slinking over the greasy surface from boulder to boulder, the Mystery Club skirted downstream of Justin, heading for cover. Once there, they crouched behind a mound of rain-smoothed rock humped like a whale.

Safe from discovery, they strained to listen. They could just separate Justin's words from the water's rush, giddy from the whirling current at their feet.

'Go on, look!' he yelled.

Rachel looked down, mesmerised and appalled.

'And I thought you had brains!' he mocked. 'Enough brains to keep quiet and to know your place.'

He spun her round to face him. He was sneering, close to her face. 'Didn't you realise you were on to a good thing? He brought you out of nowhere. Wasn't that enough?'

'Yes,' Rachel said. Her voice was calm and strong, beyond fear now. She struggled free to face Justin. 'More than enough. I'd do anything for him, you know that. Lie, keep quiet, keep you two apart, anything! But I wouldn't stand by and watch you kill him!'

'Me? How?' Justin laughed, then changed his mind. 'All right, so what? A nice quick finish, just double the dosage on his prescription. No one would know!'

'Just like the car? Just like Steve Ward and that truck he backed into a girl he'd never even seen before? No one would ever know!'

'Right again. Steve will do anything for me, for a price.' He smiled. 'Who do you think runs the best stolen luxury car racket in Yorkshire?'

'Steve Ward.' She faced him, bitter but strong.

'Right. He steals them from abroad, brings them across, re-registers them and sells them on the black market for fifty per cent less than they're worth, no questions asked. Only the best makes, mind you, no rubbish.' He took his time, enjoying the dawning look on Rachel's face. 'So when this stupid girl and her interfering buddies came along, snooping, Steve was only too happy to help me out. He's got a lot to lose, like me!'

'You never thought you'd get away with it. Not murder!'

Justin smiled again. 'I did. I am.'

'But what for?' Rachel demanded. 'You could have had the money, all of it, if only you'd waited!'

'Ah! No time, I'm afraid. I'm twenty-eight years old. I like a good time. So does Jackie.' He smiled.

'For her!' It was Rachel's turn to mock. 'You did all this for her?'

He considered it as if for the first time. 'Yes, I suppose I did!'

Rachel's anger boiled over. 'You fool!' she shouted. 'All this for her! And you'll kill me now? Go on, push me!' she taunted as he rushed at her. 'That's right! But the doctor's with Father right now. He's at the house. He'll save him. Father won't die, and you won't get the money!' She faced him, laughing bitterly above the roar of Devil's Leap. 'You can kill me and you still won't get what you want!'

Justin's rage at her words sent him wild again. He lunged at her a second time, but she sidestepped quickly. He plunged forward, losing his balance, his feet sliding from under him. The weight of his body carried him to the edge. His arms flailed and he cried out.

The girls scrambled up to the top of their rock. Rachel screamed. And then, in a second that seemed to stretch on forever, Justin toppled, slowly like a tree crashing down. He fell from the treacherous, moss-covered rocks of Devil's Leap into the mighty black current below.

16   Rescue?

Holly stood fast as Justin fell. Belinda ran forward to grab Rachel, hearing Tracy call, 'Watch out for the rocks!' For a second of horrified fascination they stood and watched Devil's Leap claim its latest victim.

Justin bounced like a puppet, his arms flung wide. The dark shape whirled amongst the wild, white eddies. The pale face turned upwards to the dark sky, the mouth open in an inaudible cry, then vanished.

Horrified, the girls struggled to gain control of their fear. 'Over here!' Holly waved them back to her position downstream of the narrow channel where Justin had fallen. In spite of everything, she couldn't just stand by and watch him die.

'This is roughly where he'll come up!' She gazed down at the current, saw where it boiled and twisted out of the funnel of rock. The others joined her, breaths held, Rachel weeping hysterically.

170

Holly squatted and inched her way close to the edge. She beckoned Belinda down next, feeling the cold spray against her face. 'Here, hold on to my wrist!' Then she ordered Tracy and Rachel to form a human chain up the sloping rock.

'Is there anything to hang on to up there?' She needed an anchor. Seconds ticked by, and still Devil's Leap refused to deliver up its victim. Holly strained her eyes to see.

At last Rachel's voice replied. 'A tree! It's not very strong, but I think I can hold on to it!'

'Do it!' Holly yelled, just as a shape like an arm bobbed to the surface. 'Hold on tight!' she screamed above the rush of the water. She leaned out, letting Belinda take her weight, and prayed. She clutched the object, slimy and rough.

It was only the branch of a tree ripped from its trunk. It tumbled into the current again as Holly let it go. She was suspended above the white foam, hoping the others could hold on. She knew the current must still be dragging Justin down, many metres deep, opening into great underwater caverns and chambers.

'Oh, please save him!' Rachel wailed. 'It'll break his father's heart!'

Belinda hung on to Holly for dear life.

'Yes!' Holly shouted at last. This time she

was right. The helpless body surfaced at last. She strained to reach. She touched the sleeve of the jacket, just as it swung out of reach. Then the water eased it back in her direction, face uppermost. She grabbed again, managing to hook her wrist around its elbow. She felt the tug and pull of mighty currents below the surface. 'I've got him!' Holly shouted. 'But you'll have to pull like crazy! Go on, *pull*!'

The four of them set all their strength against the force of the water and the dead weight of Justin's body. The sinews of Holly's arms strained, and a terrible pain shot across her shoulders. Her legs began to shudder.

'*Pull*!' Holly cried out. If they failed, if one of them let go, she was dead too. The water mocked her with its playful, treacherous eddies. 'Don't let go!'

They pulled. Slowly, inch by inch, they eased Justin out of the water. A fraction at a time they were able to stagger backwards from the edge and pull him clear. Holly hung on. She dragged him on to the rock, then collapsed over him, exhausted.

'Is he dead?' Tracy asked, afraid of the answer.

Rachel came and bent over him, feeling his wrist for a pulse. 'He's alive!' she said.

They stripped his jacket while Rachel gave mouth to mouth resuscitation. She pushed down on Justin's chest with all her might. Choking sounds told them he was reviving. Soon he breathed normally. Silently, they carried him back to the car, still unconscious.

Rachel got them all into Justin's car and drove swiftly into town. She took the riverside route, straight to the hospital. The Mystery Club supervised Justin, keeping him warm with a blanket from the boot. They watched for signs of consciousness, but there were none.

When they arrived in the forecourt, Tracy sprang out of the car and ran ahead through the double doors. She brought nurses running. Then it was out of the terrible dark night into hospital brightness.

Two uniformed figures lifted Justin on to a stretcher, and wheeled him through the gleaming glass and steel entrance. The girls and Rachel stood there in silence.

Then Doctor Goodwin was walking swiftly up to Rachel, and Kurt and Simon and others were arriving, and everyone was putting comforting hands on them, saying everything would be all right now. Old Mr Mason would recover; they'd brought him straight down to the hospital and put him on a heart monitor. New drugs would put him right. He was sleeping now.

Rachel smiled and cried, holding Holly's hand. 'Thank you!' she said over and over. 'Thank you!'

Holly's mother was there, with Mr and Mrs Hayes. They'd heard all about it from Simon. They'd been worried out of their minds. Mrs Adams hugged her daughter.

Holly looked over her mother's shoulder at the scene around her. Belinda, glasses in hand, was wrapped in hospital blankets, sipping the tea her mother had brought. She was smiling shyly at Simon. Kurt had his arm round Tracy's shoulder. The whole story was being told. They were warm and dry and safe. Justin was alive, they said, thanks to Holly.

Holly shrugged and smiled at her father as he came rushing in, screening his eyes from the white light. 'We're all right,' she told him. 'No need to worry.'

After all the danger, it took time to relax, to let the world stop spinning. Holly felt her father's arm round her shoulder and she smiled gratefully at her mother.

Jamie's head popped up close by. 'Did you get him, Holly?' he asked. 'Did he confess? Will he go to prison?'

174

Holly smiled. 'We did. Yes, yes, and yes!' Justin had condemned himself there at the water's edge. There were three impartial witnesses: herself, Tracy and Belinda.

'Well done,' Tracy's mother told them all. 'That's some criminal you just rescued!'

As if to confirm it, the police arrived in a blare of sirens, their blue uniforms spilling into the waiting room, their faces stern and efficient.

Jamie's eyes grew rounder as he looked from them to his sister. For once he was speechless.

And Holly looked across at Belinda and Tracy in a blaze of triumph. She gave them a brilliant smile and a thumbs up. One more for the Mystery Club!

FORBIDDEN ISLAND

by Fiona Kelly

Holly, Belinda and Tracy are back in the third thrilling adventure in the Mystery Club series, published by Knight Books.

1 Mysterious lights

'OK girls,' Mr Adams said as he pulled in to the kerb. 'This is it. Out you get.' He looked across at Holly. 'Apologise to your aunt for me. Tell her I can't stay. I've got an appointment to see a client at four o'clock. And, Holly . . .'

'Yes, Dad?'

'Try not to get yourself involved in any more scrapes, do you mind?'

Holly's eyes widened. 'Me? I don't get myself involved. It just happens.'

Mr Adams gave a wry smile. 'Holly, you attract trouble like a magnet. Will you try – just for this week?' He heaved a mock sigh. 'Carole didn't know what she was letting herself in for when she said she'd take you three for the holidays.'

'Don't worry, Mr Adams,' said Belinda. 'I, for one, don't intend to do anything more exciting than lying on the beach. I'll keep them under control. Trust me.'

Mr Adams laughed. He knew it was unlikely Belinda would be able to control his lively fifteen-year-old daughter. It would be like a snail trying to control a grasshopper. 'Right. Have a good time, then. See you next week.'

The three girls got their bags out of the back of the car and waved him goodbye. Tall and pretty in a blue striped tracksuit, Holly walked briskly up the path, her light brown hair bouncing in the breeze.

'Hang on a minute.' Tracy stopped to tuck her violin case more securely under her arm, then shifting her sports bag over to her other hand, she caught up with her friend in a couple of strides.

As usual, Belinda brought up the rear. Polishing her spectacles on the sleeve of her faded green sweatshirt, she picked up her case and trailed along behind them. She reached the front door just as Holly rang the bell for the second time.

'Try again,' Tracy suggested after a few moments without a reply.

Belinda shook her head. 'No point. She's got a car, hasn't she?'

'A car? Yes. Why?' Holly's grey eyes were puzzled.

'Look at the garage. No way could she keep a

car in there. It's falling apart. And no car in the drive. So, she must be out.'

Holly and Tracy exchanged glances. There were times when Belinda seemed to hit the nail on the head without even trying.

'OK, Miss Private Eye,' Tracy kidded, 'what now?'

Belinda shrugged. 'Don't ask me. It's Holly's aunt.'

'Let's go round the back. She may have left a note or something,' Tracy suggested.

But the back of the house was securely locked up, and there was no sign of a note anywhere.

Holly frowned. 'That's weird. She knew we were coming. You'd think she'd be here.'

'Perhaps she's gone out to get some bread or something,' Tracy said.

Holly shook her head. 'More likely to have gone to see a house.'

'A house?'

'She's an estate agent. She used to be in a big office in York, but now she's got her own business here in Framley. I expect someone rang up and she didn't want to leave it till tomorrow in case the other agency gets it. There're only the two of them in Framley and the competition's really keen.'

'There's a window open upstairs,' Tracy said.

Belinda dumped her bag and sprawled out on one of the patio chairs. 'Well, you two can do what you like. I'm going to relax.' She took a Mars bar out of her bag and, tilting her head up to the warm sunshine, took a bite.

Holly and Tracy looked up at the window. It was only slightly ajar, but maybe they could reach it.

Tracy tugged at a tangle of branches that snaked their way up the wall and across a tiny balcony beneath the window. 'Think this will hold me?'

'Looks a bit brittle,' Holly said warily.

'I'm going to try.' Tracy grabbed at the trunk. The sun glinted for a moment on her short blonde hair. Then she disappeared into the canopy of leaves. Seconds later there was an ominous creaking noise and a length of tree pulled away from the wall.

'Whoops! I knew we shouldn't have had those chocolate éclairs on the drive over here,' Tracy giggled.

'Be careful,' Holly said. 'It may be one of Aunt Carole's prize plants.'

From her vantage point above them, Tracy looked around. 'Judging by the state of the garden, she's got too many prize plants. You couldn't fit another plant in anywhere. Anyway, which do you care more about – her prize plants or your best friend's life?'

'Get on with it.' Holly grinned.

A few minutes later Tracy was on the balcony, and from there it didn't take long to get the window open and climb inside. 'I won't be long,' she called down. 'Meet you at the front porch.'

When the door opened, Tracy looked impressed. 'This place is bigger than it looks. And the view is amazing . . . You can see for miles. There's an island in the bay. Think we could hire a boat and have a look?'

Holly pushed past her. 'I doubt it. Aunt Carole told me it's not allowed. I don't know why.'

'Well, there's someone there now. I saw lights flashing.'

'Probably just the sun reflecting off some glass or something. Anyway, now we're here I'll show you the bedrooms.'

Belinda and Tracy followed Holly up the two flights of stairs to what had once been the servants' quarters. In contrast to the spaciousness of her aunt's room on the first floor, all three bedrooms on this level were tiny, with sloping ceilings and windows that jutted out into the roof. But they were fully fitted, and furnished in bold, dramatic colours, each with its own washbasin. There was also a bathroom and shower as well as a tiny sitting-room with television and stereo all on the same level.

'Fantastic,' Tracy said admiringly. 'It's just like having your own apartment. If this was my family I'd be down here every weekend.'

Just then, they heard the crunch of tyres on gravel and the slam of a car door. 'That'll be her,' Holly said. 'Come on.'

They ran downstairs, and were in the hall as Aunt Carole opened the door.

'I'm so sorry, girls,' she said. 'I meant to be home ages ago, but I got delayed.'

'You didn't mind us coming in before you got home, did you?' Holly asked.

'Of course not.' She looked vaguely round, as if she'd lost something. Holly noticed that her hands were shaking, and that there two high spots of colour in her cheeks, as if she had been having a furious row. *Strange*, thought Holly. *Aunt Carole is usually so cool and laid back.*

'You haven't met my friends,' Holly said. 'This is Belinda Hayes. And this is Tracy Foster. She's half American. I wrote to you about them, when I started the Mystery Club.'

'Hi.' Tracy smiled, but Aunt Carole didn't seem to notice.

'Sorry. I've had a bad day. Let me have a shower and change, then I'll be human again.

Help yourself to whatever you want in the fridge. I'll be back.'

Belinda and Tracy exchanged glances as she hurried past and up the stairs.

Holly's cheeks reddened. She tried to cover up her embarrassment. 'Like she said, she's had a bad day. Oh, well, let's see what there is to eat.'

By the time Aunt Carole reappeared they had made some toasted sandwiches and were sitting in front of the TV.

'That's better,' she said. 'Sorry I was so prickly before. I had a bit of a brush with another estate agent.'

Within minutes they were laughing and chatting together, the earlier awkwardness forgotten. 'So, Holly . . . tell me about the Mystery Club.'

Holly's eyes glowed. There was nothing she liked better than talking about the Mystery Club. 'Well, you know how lonely I was when we first moved to Willow Dale? I didn't know anyone there, and it's really difficult starting in a new school right in the middle of a school year . . .'

Her aunt nodded sympathetically.

'Anyway, I put an advert in the school newspaper to see if anyone else was interested in mystery stories. And these two turned up.'

She grinned round at Tracy and Belinda.

'They didn't know much about mysteries when we first started – well, none of us did, in a way. But you'd be surprised what's turned up since then.'

'So your father tells me,' Aunt Carole said dryly. 'Some of them more exciting than you expected, I gather.'

Holly smiled. 'A bit,' she admitted.

Carole turned to Tracy. 'And you're from America, Holly says.'

'Yeah, California. But I've been in England since I was twelve. I came back with Mom when my parents got divorced. We've lived in Willow Dale ever since.'

'She's brilliant at virtually everything. Games . . . music . . . You name it she can do it,' Holly put in. 'I reckon she'll be in the Olympics one day.'

Tracy reddened. 'Don't believe her, Miss Earnshaw. Holly's practising to be a journalist. And if she can't find interesting facts to write about she makes them up as she goes along.'

Aunt Carole laughed. 'She's always been the same. That's what makes her so good at detective work. By the way, I've got a copy of a new mystery novel for you, Holly. Are you interested?'

'You bet! Thanks.'

'And, girls . . . skip the Miss Earnshaw bit. I'm Carole, right?'

'Right.'

They had just finished the evening meal and were clearing the dishes into the kitchen when a car's headlights swept the windows. Seconds later, the doorbell rang furiously.

Carole was in the middle of loading the dishwasher. Before she had time to go to the door, the bell rang again.

Holly raised an eyebrow. *Someone* was in a hurry. 'Go ahead,' she said. 'We'll finish off here.'

Hastily the three friends cleared the rest of the table, listening with unease at the raised voices in the hallway. Then, as Holly took out the last few plates, the living-room door burst open and a tall, heavily-built man in his mid-thirties strode angrily into the room.

Ignoring Holly completely, he turned to face Carole who had followed him in. 'And another thing,' he continued, 'Wetherby's Farm is *our* market property. Don't think you can muscle in and take our custom.'

'Mr Hare,' Carole replied coolly, 'don't rush to conclusions. I didn't "muscle in". That property has been on the market for six months, and what have you done about it? Nothing. This afternoon Mrs Wetherby phoned me and I went there to value it. You can't expect her to sit around and wait for you for ever. If I can't do better than you I'll eat my hat!'

You tell him, Holly thought.

'You're a newcomer here,' he snarled. 'You've only been in Framley for six months. Bingley and Hare have been here for sixty years.'

'Oh, really?' Carole replied sweetly. 'I didn't think you were that old.'

The man's colour deepened. He looked as if he would explode at any minute.

Holly took out the plates, and leaned against the kitchen door, grinning.

'No need to worry about Carole,' she said. 'She's an expert at putting people in their place.'

By the time they had finished loading the dishwasher and clearing up the kitchen, the man had left.

'All clear,' Carole said, popping her head round the door. 'Thank you for taking over. Now we can have our coffee in peace.'

'What was all that about?' asked Holly, as they took in the coffee on a tray.

'That's Mr High-and-Mighty Hare. Junior partner in the only other estate agency in Framley. Old Mr Bingley's all right. I get on well with him, but he's more or less retired. He only comes in a couple of times a week. This one thinks he owns the place.' She sighed. 'I won't go into details. I've just got a weird feeling that there's more to this set-up than meets the eye.'

'Tell us,' said Holly, intrigued.

Her aunt hesitated. 'It doesn't sound much when you put it into words. It may not be anything, really. But somehow . . . when I went to see Mrs Wetherby at the farm today I felt as though something sinister was going on.' She paused again.

'Sinister? Why?' Holly's grey eyes sparkled. If there was anything to raise her interest it was the thought of something sinister going on.

'Well . . . Mrs Wetherby's a widow, and she's got a farm down on Fram Bight . . .'

'Fram *what*?' Tracy giggled. 'You English sure have got some funny names.'

'Not bite, as in B-I-T-E,' Carole laughed. 'Bight as in bend in the coast. It's where the land loops out into the sea. Anyway, it's an isolated place. Only Framley Grange, the farm – and, of course, the island. Yet Mrs Wetherby is convinced that there are strange people hanging around. She said she's seen flashing lights in the night . . . tyres churning up the mud between the farm and the jetty . . . that sort of thing.' She sighed.

'I don't know how much is true and how much is her imagination. At her age it could be either.'

'I've seen the lights she's talking about,' Tracy said. 'They were coming from the island. This afternoon. When I climbed into your bedroom.'

Carole looked puzzled. 'That's impossible. No one's allowed on the island. It was used for experiments in germ warfare during the Second World War. Anthrax, I think. It's still lethal. You must have been mistaken. Perhaps it was a fishing boat in the bay.'

Holly was impatient to hear the rest of the story. 'Never mind about the lights. What else happened?'

'I told her to ring Bingley and Hare to let them know she had appointed me as her agent as well. Martyn Hare asked to speak to me, and he was really rude. Well, you heard him, so you can guess. Anyway, Mrs Wetherby is convinced that most of the things that are happening are to do with the new owners of Framley Grange. They're a couple of brothers, Thomas and Ian Clough. I thought I might pop in to see them in a day or two to see what it's all about.'

'Can we come?' Holly asked.

Carole shook her head. 'Sorry. Not for that sort of thing. I'll take you down there if you like. You can explore while I talk to them.'

They had to accept that for the time being, though Holly didn't like taking no for an answer. After all, why miss all the fun if there was some way of getting in on the act?

Before they went to bed that night, Holly called a meeting of the Mystery Club in the sitting-room upstairs. Moonlight filtered through the diamond-shaped panes of the window, patterning the carpet like a giant jigsaw, and the three sat in the glow of the gas-fire, talking.

'Why should that Martyn Hare be so miffed about Carole trying to sell the farm?' Holly mused. 'He's had six months to have a go.'

Belinda looked up from a copy of *Horse and Hound* that she'd found a shelf. She was absolutely mad about everything to do with horses. 'Maybe he thinks women belong at home. Not at work, competing with men.'

Holly grinned. 'You could be right.'

'I wouldn't mind having a look at this Bight place tomorrow,' Tracy said. 'How far is it, Holly?'

'I'm not actually sure. I've only stayed here once before – and that was when Mum and I came up for a couple of days to give Carole a hand to move in.'

'That explains it,' Tracy said. 'I wondered why

you didn't say anything about the island and the germ warfare. It's a bit spooky, really. And what about the lights and things?'

'I think you're making a mystery out of nothing,' Belinda interrupted. 'There's probably a perfectly normal explanation. Anyway, I'm off to bed.' And, tucking the magazine under her arm, she ambled out.

'Typical!' Tracy laughed. 'Give her a horse magazine, and you've lost her completely.'

But before Holly had a chance to comment, there was a shout from Belinda's room. 'Hey! Come and look. Quick!'

Holly and Tracy rushed into the other room. Belinda was standing by the window. The moon shone down brightly out of a cloudless arch of sky. The island, a dark silhouette on the horizon, looked entirely deserted but for flickering shafts of light – white, then green, then white, then red.

And from the mainland came an answering signal. One . . . two . . . three green, and a longer flash of white.